700
Block

JAMES FREEMAN

ISBN: 0692262857
ISBN-13: 978-0692262856

DEDICATION

To hard work, determination, knowing thyself and to my
grandmother Vietta Freeman

CONTENTS

ACKNOWLEDGMENTS

I want to give a few shout-outs to my brothers Nick Gay aka GK, Tony Gay aka Tone, Chauncey aka Lil GK, my big brothers Dewann and Dewayne Bulls, my bothers Dana Patton, Tyree Atkinson, Charles Jay aka Pedro RIP bro, to my sister Tracey Freeman, my mom Linda Freeman, my dad Nicky Gay, my aunt Angela Gay, my cousin Hamin Gray aka habeeb, my cousin Jamal Gray, my aunt Katie Freeman, my aunt Regina Freeman, to my cousin Robin Freeman RIP cuz, to my cousin Rudy Freeman and Rudy Freeman Jr. RIP big cuz and lil cuz, to my cousin Chico Loc RIP cuz, to my cuz C-Wic RIP cuz, to my cousin Quinton Gay and my aunt Patricia Gray, to my cousins Matt, Kenny, Tia & Lexy Fitzgerald and their dad Kenny Fitzgerald and aunt Teresa, to my lil cousins Magnolia Wop, Ty Murder, Muzz, Mutter Butt, my cousin Michael Clark RIP, Lunchmeat RIP, my cuz Keen Low and anyone else from all over I missed that fucks with me mad love. To Haneef Taylor from South West Philly, who was my editor, hold your head up player. And I saved the best for last to my wife Denise Freeman I love you baby, thanks for everything and all the support you gave me on everything, you're the best.

CHAPTER 1

As a young child I was full of energy and hateful thoughts. My mom always told me I would never be anything. But at them stages in my life I never paid her no mind. My mom, Reida, was a crack head so me and my brother TJ never really had any food to eat or any good looking clothes to wear. People at school always tried to clown us so we stayed in fights and always got kicked out of school. One day me and my brother got into a fight about who looks the best. When I look back at it now, it was so dumb trying to impress them dumbass girls. Then when the punches rang out, my eye was black and I busted my brother's lip, the girls said ya'll both look ugly now. We beat them up so they could look ugly too. That day we swore to each other that we would never fight again and stay tight like brothers should. On the way home, me and my bro walked and talked about so many things. The one thing he said to me stuck in my head forever. He said "L-Roy I'm trying to get rich and get mom out of Pittsburgh because she keep smoking that stuff and I just want her to

stop." Then he started crying. Now TJ was younger than me only by two years but it made things rough for me because I had to take care of my younger brother. I held him close as we continued to walk up the steps to the house.

It was around twelve and mom was high and screaming at me and TJ about coming in so late. I wasn't trying to hear it, neither was TJ, so we ran up to the room and locked the door. That was the only safe spot in the house because my mom sold everything even herself. I stayed up most of the night thinking about the future and what I was going to do to get my family out the hood. The next morning me and TJ went to Aunt Matty's house to get something to eat. Now Aunt Matty was a pure hoe, she was fine and really wasn't my Aunt. She was only related to us through my uncle, a pimp named Art. They had a son together named Mark. When I looked at Ms Matty I was always saying dag she thick, now I was young but I knew what a good looking woman was and my Uncle Art knew how to pick them. But what made me like her was she always had something skimpy on where you could see her body and she was always bending over so you could see her big butt with no panties on and her big breasts with nipples that stayed hard. She could kill and she would always tease us. One time, we caught her having sex and we just watched. We never told Mark me and TJ kept it to ourselves. Mark was lighter than me and TJ, almost looked white with his curly hair and long eyelashes. We said if he grew boobs we would call him Miss.

So we grubbed then ran off throwing rocks at cars, houses, dogs, and people whatever we thought was funny

to hit. We did this all day then we took Mark home and asked Ms Matty could we stay the night because we didn't want to go back to the "hell house" as we liked to call it. We knew Mark's mom would say yeah and when she did I was happy. That night all three of us stayed up playing games, we passed out and I woke up about 2pm. everyone else in the house was asleep except Ms Matty. I made my way up the steps that's when and saw someone in the bathroom; the door was cracked so I snuck a peek. It was Mark's mom in the shower with the shower curtain open.

I never saw her completely naked up and close. I just drooled at how thick she was, her ass was so round and soft looking that every time she moved it jiggled, her stomach was flat as the floor, breasts big and round like melons with nipples longer than my finger nails. I never really saw a woman's vagina up close. Hers was bushy like a small fro but neat looking and when she picked up her leg I started getting hard because her pussy was so fat. That's when it happened, she looked right at me and winked. I ran off with my heart beating a million times a minute. I didn't say a word to nobody. It was wonderful the prettiest woman I've ever seen I just saw naked and she winked at me and smiled. I said to myself when I get older I would get her and treat her good.

When Mark and TJ woke up, I was chillin watching TV thinking about Ms Matty, My Matty. When Mark came back in with a water jug and threw water on me and screamed April Fools. I said to myself that's not how you play April fools jokes and before he knew what happened, me & TJ were beating the life out of him. His mom ran to break it up and said we could not come back for one week.

So me & TJ went down our friend Sheena's house to chill, her sister Sharon was in the room giving me dirty looks like she wanted to fight or something. We didn't get along at all ever since we were six and we were playing hide and go get it I was only supposed to get a few kisses and a few humps but I kissed her and tried to stick my finger in her butt and finger it. I wasn't in there more than 10 seconds before she started to trip and started going crazy on me like girls do. When I sat down, I said hi to Sharon but she just turned her head. I didn't care as long as she wasn't trying to sneak me with any weapons. Then Sharon took some of her moms gin and juice and her dad's cigars.

We were gone in a matter of minutes, acting a fool, trying to do everything but we couldn't move one foot. That's when I said to myself this must be how that crack make my mom feel. It really didn't matter to me that she was smoking, it's what she did to get the drug. I was always upset about something, mainly life, and I was always ready to show it when I drank even as a youngin I could act real crazy. When I finally said it was time for me to go home, it was the next day and TJ didn't want to leave so I left him there. I said I will take the blues from my mom when I get home but my mom had company so I was saved. I knew that whoever she was with, she was trying to get their money. I just knocked and said I was home. My mom said "Boy where is your brother at?" I told her he was at Aunt Matty's house, that's where we both were but he wasn't trying to come home. I just got quiet and I went to my room turned up the radio and looked out the window.

CHAPTER 2

"Sheena, tell TJ mom said he has to go."

"But Sharon, its dark outside and L-Roy ain't come back yet."

"I'm not going to say nothing but don't let mom catch you."

"Alright."

Sharon goes back upstairs and tells her mom that Sheena won't kick TJ out. Meanwhile downstairs Sheena is telling TJ how much she likes him but TJ ain't really feeling what she's saying. Then they heard footsteps' sounding her mother's getting louder and closer. She wasn't paying it no mind then her mom walks down the basement steps screaming.

"Boy if you don't get up and take your young behind home, I'm a treat you like one of mine and your mom will

have to just be mad at me."

"Ms. Victoria, I ain't even trying to."

"Get out."

"But mom Sharon said that you told her you wasn't going to put him out."

"But nothing take your fast ass upstairs. Bye TJ they'll see you tomorrow."

"Bye Ms. Victoria."

TJ shuts the door and says to himself, let me get my hike on Ms. V be tripping. He is walking down the street paying no attention to the cars flying around Mount Pleasant and he just steps out in the street and he gets hit by a car so hard they said it looked like he could fly.

I'm looking out the window and wondering what all them sirens are for so I went outside and seen all these people on Mount Pleasant. I decided to walk down, I only lived at the beginning of Chicago Street, so I could see everything. When I got closer and pushed through the crowd, I heard people screaming. "No that's TJ not L-Roy"

Me and my bro look so much alike even though we had different dads. When I seen TJ on the stretcher I tried to talk to him but he was unconscious and slipped into a coma at the hospital. I ran up to my mom's room and told her what happened and that's the first time I ever saw her come out of one of them trances that crack heads be in

and the first time I seen pain in my mom's eyes like she really cared. My mom got ready and we got a ride down to Allegheny General Hospital from my god sister Angel who loves me with all her heart but she was so fat and smelly.

When we arrived at the hospital we got all the information on where my little brother was and that he was in critical condition. I just kept shaking my head. He had a blood clot and they had to amputate his leg. He was in a coma for two years and all we did was come down, pray for him and hold his hand. My mom was crying over TJ and saying she would do anything to get her baby back while she was throwing the old flowers and replacing them with new ones.

The trauma it brought to the family still did some good. My mom didn't steal out the house no more and she gave crack up. I was proud but she sits in her room a lot and don't say nothing to nobody while she smokes on her joints and sip her Wild Irish Rose looking at the walls crying asking why. Meanwhile I'm back in school trying to do good, making B's and C's and even some A's. I still ain't got the best looking clothes but I managed.

One day I was at the hospital with my mom TJ's hand moved. We were trying to talk to him but he wouldn't say nothing. For about a week he just kept moving his hand and my mom said God will bless us baby, he's going to bless you baby. I just walked around the hospital getting chips and different snacks to eat just to keep me moving. I hated that my bro had to be in that dumbass bed and had to get his leg cut off. It did something to me. One night I stayed back while mama went home, I wasn't supposed to

7

be there but I stayed anyways because I love my brother and would do anything for him. I was sitting there talking to him about my problems even if he couldn't talk back. That's when he blinked his eyes then kept blinking them. I kept talking and he just looked at me.

"L-Roy what's wrong, why are you looking at me like that and where am I?"

I just looked at him like he was a ghost. He got up and he seen one of his legs were gone and asked me what happened. I was still froze and couldn't talk then he pushed me.

"L-Roy why am I in the hospital?"

"You got hit by a car on Mount Pleasant and had to get your leg cut off because it was balled up and you've been in a coma for two years and a couple weeks."

He just started crying so I called my mom and she got a ride down.

We took him home and told him about everything. TJ got SSI and that helped out a lot because we needed it. I was growing up fast and I was bad as hell. TJ had a fake leg and was getting around pretty good.TJ was bad too but mom watched over him.

I always stayed in a car, it didn't matter if it was stolen or car jacked with a knife. I was pretty tall for my age so a lot of people were already scared of my hook that I got down to a tee. TJ was always in the way and it took him a long time to run fast enough to get away from 5-0. One day I caught some old lady slippin in this Benz on Federal

Street. As soon as she opened the door, I grabbed her by her hair, took her purse and keys then threw her on the ground and me and TJ was out. TJ was my dog, we did everything together. We had that Benz for about three weeks flying around and doing donuts in it. The Jakes hopped on us on Penfort Street, that's in the hood up Northview Heights. We bolted on them, we hit a right, heading across the bridge and then across Perrysville onto Charles Street all downhill. Halfway down the hill I tell my little bro I'm a jump out then I jumped. The car kept going and hit a pole while my little brother was still in it. His reaction time was so slow. I head up the city steps on Wilson Avenue these slow ass Jakes was on me so I dogged him. I ran down this backstreet, jumped over this wooden fence and climbed over another fence. I took my coat off and threw it. I went to cross the street to the row houses on Charles Street then a female pig pulled her burner on me so I put my hands up and said I didn't do nothing that I was just going back to my house from my grandma's house. This nut let me go and I was happier than a bitch. As I'm chilling at the row houses on Charles Street and I'm looking up at the scene and I see TJ fighting with the police. I'm like damn, I knew he would get caught. So I peeped him get slammed by this Jake and I couldn't take it no more. I ran up there and put in some major work on them pigs for about 10 to 15 minutes before they started getting out on me. After they got us in the car, they took us to the jail and when we went to go see the Judge I took all the charges so they would let TJ go.

CHAPTER 3

The placement they sent me to was a hellhole and I hated that shit even though I only did 12 months it felt like forever and some. My first day in placement I came in at night but the dudes were still up. Dudes from Philly and from Cleveland but the Burg was thick and we were rowdier then any of them other cities. Even if we were outmanned, we had heart and no one could take that from us. Not even the punk ass staff who always try to act tough but I gave them fear.

Once we were talking that gang shit, for the most part dudes were scared because we had no fear, and was fighting pigs and jumping them too. If you weren't with us and you weren't from Pittsburgh we were going to give you the blues and we didn't care, riots, fistfights and everything else went down even weapons. Whether prepared or snuck it didn't matter we stuck together. A few times them boys from Philly told the staff that we were clicked up and doing them dirty and even told them about

the blanket parties we give them on a regular. I really never had any problems with anybody from Philly but when I did it would be crazy because I always would go on beast mode, time after time I proved myself and got praises for what I done. It was always like that in placement.

I played sports like football, basketball and baseball. I even liked playing. When I think about some of them guys up in the placement, all they did was talk. Mainly them dudes from Cleveland they didn't want no problems, it was just like that.

I was going home on home passes and getting pussy was a must. I like dicking females down, I was good at it. It felt like as soon as I got home it was time for me to go back. I could've ran but I didn't want to. I like going back up there with a fresh pair of sneakers, fresh cut, a new fit, a couple hundred in my pocket, gold and ice that shines. That was the shit to all them dudes who was talking like they were getting money on the street but they coming back looking like shit. Me and my man shits on niggas squat down and shit on them fake clowns.

When it used to come close for dudes to leave, other dudes would try to act tough because they know you wanted to go home. But me I didn't give a fuck I been f.t.a before and they knew I really didn't care. If you was from the Burgh I had your back. Now it was my time to go home and dudes didn't want no problems. Sometimes they let you out before your time and that's what happened to me.

On my way home it looked crazy, we passed so many

cows and different farms. I like the city life but I would love to get a huge house in the country. As we passed ponds with schools of fish, people working in the field, ducklings following their parents and so many other animals it was crazy. I had always wondered what it would feel like to fly across the plains like an eagle or something so I dozed off with that on my mind. It was a three hour trip.

When I woke up we were in downtown Pittsburgh. We had already let them dudes off from the Eastside like them dudes from Homewood, Wilkinsburg and other little spots out on the east. Now it was time to hit the Northside, Manchester then Hoodtown and couple dudes on Wilson and Perrysville. The last stop was the hood, the people who was from there were young beasts. Northview Heights that spot and they let me off on Mount Pleasant right at the beginning. I ran straight down to seven court they also called it's 7cm short for 7 court mafia.

When I hit the bend, the block went crazy. I'd only been gone twelve months but it seemed like years. Rudy came over and said what's up. That's my old head he's cool but he thinks he's the shit and his shit don't stank if you feel what I'm saying. He did about eight years upstate after a drug deal gone bad which he had killed two people. He got convicted but he came back on it. He appealed and he knocked it. It just took eight years. He's a little dude about 5'1 5'2 but he had so much anger inside of him it made him around 7'. He loved his caddies and bright colors. Who would think in the future he would lose his life because of me. All the young bucks in the hood looked up to me they always thought I had money because I stayed in

the flyest whips but most of them were stolen. "What's cracking L-Roy?"

"What's popping Ray J?"

"Just chilling cuz holding the block down. Look, I holds it down for real cuz, " as he pulls up his shirt and shows me this all black Glock 40, while taking puffs on this blunt and trying to pass it to me.

"That's nice. But you banging now young buck?"

"Naw but I hold the hood down and ain't nobody just going to be bussing on us."

"I feel you youngin, I'm a holla at you later Ray J."

"Alright L-Roy."

And as soon as I turn back around Sheena's all in my face.

"What's up sexy ass L-Roy."

"Nothing fine Ass Sheena."

"What's the deal young buck? I know you need some pussy."

Now Sheena was a little older than me, fine as fuck and thick chubby if you know what I mean. She was like 5'6 160 but it didn't matter because them hips was sitting on dubs. Her ass wasn't that big but her hips made everything go together.

She's the only big girl I knew that had a small chest, real small but they were still cute. She had hazel eyes and

always wore her hair in a ponytail with them waves she had in there, light skin and had a big mouth so if I hit it I had to do it right. But on the up and up I really wanted Sharon she looked just like Ms. Victoria big lips, long legs, fat ass and big tits, body that's banging and she loved to work out. When she comes out to the block everyone stops what they're doing and looks at Sharon. Brown skin, brown eyes, long hair thick with curls she's a real showstopper and still a virgin but not Sheena. So on the way to the house I looked at Sharon and she didn't look away maybe it's what I had on a wife beater tight as fuck and my nipples were even showing, my arms were huge all I did was fight and lift weights so I knew I looked good. I smiled and she gave me a little grin, I was cool with that it meant we came pretty far over the years.

So on my way in I said hi to Sheena's mom she smiled and said "I know you're glad to be home boy."

"Yes ma'am."

"Okay L-Roy I will talk to you later, I'm watching my stories."

"Bye Ms. V."

We walked up the steps and went into Sheena's room, I touched on her ass while she started kissing me and playing with my dick it started growing and it hurt to leave it in my pants especially with these little ass draws on we call Superman's because they're like tights.

I told her to pull it out and when she did she bent over and start sucking on it. I was like damn this feels

good. It felt crazy because I knew I had to nut but I was trying to hold it back because if I did she might not let me hit it. But it came out anyway nice bulky load of creamy cum all in Sheena's mouth and she kept sucking and swallowed everything like a real pro. Next thing I know I'm hard again so I picked her up and start taking her clothes off, playing with her breasts the whole time then she jumped up on the bed and got on all fours.

I got right behind that ass and started pounding on that pussy since I already came I was able to keep going we were both sweating crazy. Me pounding on that ass just kept getting louder and louder and I had to come. Then I saw the door was opening and her mom popped in and peeked. So I took a few more humps, pulled out and nutted all over Sheena's butt then she turned around to start licking on my balls. She licked the first one when Ms. Victoria said "Oh that's enough you got to go now L-Roy."

As I got up I didn't hurry I wanted her mom to look at me just to let her know she couldn't get any, just to tease her. On my way downstairs Sharon said "Did you have fun? You damn sure made enough noise that's why mom came up there because she got tired of hearing Sheena screaming yes L-Roy, no L-Roy, right there L-Roy, go deeper L-Roy, I love you L-Roy. We just got tired of her saying your name."

"I'll get at you later Sharon."

"Bye little dickhead."

I closed the door and kept walking, she wanted me to start a fight with her so she could go crazy like usual. She liked me and I knew it but she didn't want to let me know.

On my way out to the street I peep this car moving real slow. Once I seen the head of who was driving I scream drive-by. That's when niggas started running and young bucks started busting because they thought they had something to prove. I fell to the ground because I've seen too many people trying to run and get hit all in their backs. Then I seen Angel, I told her to get down but it was too late she got hit and hanging limp over a railing. I just put my head down.

When it was all over everyone ran up to Angel but she was already gone. She didn't have anything to do with this bullshit out here. I called 911 but they took a while to come they always did. We followed the ambulance down to the hospital in Rudy's caddy. TJ showed up and asked me why didn't I come get him when I first came home, I told him I was fucking Sheena he just laughed.

The doc came out said "she was already dead but we saved the kids."

"The kids?" my mom said "What kids? She wasn't pregnant."

"Ma'am she was pregnant with twin girls."

I just walked away.

Me and TJ jumped in this ride he got from some drug dealer for holding drugs for him in his fake leg incase task

force ran up. It was a two-door Honda Accord it was gray with leather seats. It was nice, had a sound system and it was fast. Me and TJ drove around all day smoking dro in these wraps he had. I like the strawberry ones. TJ was sitting on a few stacks, he was working for our uncle Art. Art was giving him ounces and telling him to give him back 600 so TJ was killing em. TJ gave me 500 to put my pocket then stopped the car and told me this pound of weed was mine. It was regular but it still was a good look. He told me uncle Art would look out for me. I said cool but I didn't feel like going over there right now so we just kept riding around plus I didn't really like uncle Art he was a lame. He had all that money but he didn't give Mark, none of the women he was fucking or the kids he had by them a dime. That's why I stayed away from him but I never told him that. I thought I would need him for something, he had millionaire status in the hood and he was my uncle so I never said anything.

"L-Roy, L-Roy, what's up bro you always in lala land."

"Naw TJ I'm just chilling."

"Uncle Art said if I keep doing good he would give me 4 1/2 ounces."

"That's what's up bro."

"What's the matter L-Roy?"

"Angel's dead bro."

"I know but you got to let it go L-Roy. We need this money remember."

"Yeah but there got to be another way TJ."

"Let me find out you scared bro."

"It ain't about being scared, I been tired of this shit."

"It a be alright big bro."

I was always hateful of the way the world was because black people was always trying to outdo each other even when they really didn't have anything. Just like crabs in a bucket when you on your way out they pulling you back down. If black folks just stuck together the anger I have wouldn't have even been there. TJ and I went to the Hill or Hill district it's another spot in the Burgh that get plenty of money.

As soon as we hit Center Avenue fiends was running up from everywhere. I told TJ let me see the Mac and got out the ride and told them give us some room because with fiends you always have to be careful if they think your weak the gonna get you and since TJ's leg was gone he don't fight and I respect that. TJ smashed a half an ounce in about five minutes it always bang like that on the hill and on the Northside. Flue Diz was on the block. TJ spotted him first.

"Yo Flue Diz, What's cracking nigga?"

"Just chilling homey. I know it ain't that nigga L-Roy. What's the deal baby?"

"Chillin."

"L-Roy, yo dog you got big as hell b."

"Naw Flue it ain't about nothing."

"Shits pimpin, I can't get that big and I see you still crazy then a motha fucka wit the mac out broad daylight L-Roy."

"Fam you know these fiends on the hill could get crazy especially when they think you sweet."

"I smell you L. TJ let me hold something I'm trying to come up like you baby. Shit TJ everybody knows ya Uncle Art eaten crazy and that's who you fucking with you know the streets talk b."

"Flue, you see that bitch ass nigga shady?'

"Naw, he been ducked off B."

"What you playing wit flue?"

"T I aint got shit but a quey and about 300 in the cut and some sticky about two maybe three blunts of that."

Now Flue Diz was a cool nigga, I met him in placement. We watched each other's back and I said I would get at him when I got out. He's a tall skinny nigga about 6'8 black as night and had a long ass beard.

"Look flue, I'm a give you this pound of weed my bro gave me, just give me 800 back."

"No doubt."

"Here I'm a get at you later, and if you see that nigga shady split his wig for me and you won't have to pay me

nothing."

"Alright B. I'm a get up on y'all later."

"TJ spin the block them Jakes look like they watch in us."

"Naw man this the money spot, they always watching dudes, they ain't worried bout us. You just trippin."

As soon as he said that they pulled right up on us asking my brother for his driver's license but my little bro had it. Then he start trying to ask me stuff, I told him get out my face I'm chilling then he told us to get out of the car. My bro act like he was about to open the door when I closed it. "What's the matter with you are you fucking crazy?"

"Man lock the door, roll your window up, start the car up and let's be out."

His partner jumped out of the cop car and says "turn the car off and get out now the both of you".

I screamed "man we ain't getting out of nothing we didn't do shit."

So he drew his gat and said "turn the car off and get out."

"TJ run that nigga over."

"Man I'm not hitting no cop."

"If you would of fucking did what I said bro we got all the shit on us and I just got out."

"Turn the car off and get out with your hands up."

"Wait bitch you ain't gonna to be rushing us." "Bro get out and when you see me punch dude duck because they comin and I ain't going back to jail."

So we got out of the car dude came right to me because he didn't like how it's talking to him. He pushed me up against the car I didn't say nothing because I already knew what I was going to do, I looked at TJ he just smiled and so did I. I have the Mac in front of me and TJ had the coke under his nuts about an eight ball. As soon as he touched me, I sidestepped to the left and unloaded one of my best hooks of all time dropping him fast then I pulled with my right hand. It happened so fast that TJ took too long to duck and I had to aim at the pigs head so I didn't hit TJ. I hit him in the face with so many rounds that his face didn't even look real and TJ said that's the first time he seen brains.

I shot the cop on the ground making sure he was dead. The other cop had died with his gun in his hand getting off one round. Their backup didn't get there in time, we were already gone and almost back to the heights. TJ had blood all over him from that dumbass cop. Damn I said why couldn't they had just left us the fuck alone. That was the first time I had killed anybody but it wouldn't be the last in this web of destruction I was caught in.

CHAPTER 4

The nightmares I had were crazy, I had them for weeks and I couldn't stay asleep. I kept seeing myself in shootouts with the police and they just kept following me everywhere I went and everybody I knew was a pig of some sort besides my brother TJ. He's the only one I talk to. They never said anything about me or TJ in the news I just knew we were done. So I told TJ don't tell nobody. About a month went by that's when I started going back outside. My mind was always in deep thought and I always was thinking about doing something to somebody.

I was on the block one day when a platinum colored Acura pulled up on me fast, I pulled out the mac and was about to spray when my man B-Real stuck his head out the ride.

"You gonna shoot the kid now?"

"Naw but you scared the shit out of me Real."

"Come on cuz let's head to the other side."

"No doubt pimpin."

"Get in the ride and lock the door L, niggas be trying to carjack around ya way homey."

"So I heard you on something light b."

"Something light, come out the Stead and I promise you'll double your money."

"Get the fuck out of here b it ain't biting like that."

"Man it's biting like that more than the side b."

"Naw not like the side but the prices are different L"

"What you mean fam?"

"Like a dime is 20 if you sell weight oz is 1200 and so forth, stamp bags are 40 bucks a piece."

"I smell you now b."

"See L I only fuck with dope and pills, x pills b for sure they bang out here 25 to 30 bucks a pill."

"What! They are 10 to 15 bucks on the side B. Tell me fam where do I sign. Hold on cuz. Let me answer this call."

"Yo, What's crackin TJ?"

"Where you at L-Roy?"

"With B Real out the stead trying to get this money shit

bubblin."

"Put Real on."

"Here Real it's TJ."

"What's up stunna?"

"What's up real?"

"Paperchasen baby, look TJ you got to come through"

"I'll be out there in a couple I'm handling some business right now."

"Alright, holla"

"Here cuz."

"Yo L I'll see you in a few."

"Yo real I need one of these young broad's crib to post up at."

"I already got that handled."

We rode up on W. 13th St. to some chick named Tony. Tony was a skinny sick looking chick who was eating. She had like five rides outside, the best one was the range and the worst one was this 96 Lex she had all rimmed up with smoke black windows. She came out said hi to me, gave me a hug then took me inside. B Real said he'll be back later. I just put up the black power fist as he drove off.

She talked to me for a while, she was pretty but just

sickly skinny. She played music while we drank on that Hen. It was only around 2 o'clock so we had all day. Her phone rang. "Hold on one minute L"

"What's up?"

"Tony I need something for about 200"

"Alright come on up unk."

Unk was a word the used for male fiends an aunty was the word they used for female fiends.

"Yo L you got something for 200."

I thought to myself ain't she on but I didn't say nothing I just gave her 20 stones and she said that's too much and gave me 10 back. I had already forgot about what B Real had told me. It went like that all day and I forgot about TJ. I asked her aint she on she told me she like to see men eat.

"I'm who put B Real on but he scared of me that's why he ain't my man. I already knew who you are and I told him to go and get you when he said he knew you."

That night she gave me head all night and she didn't even want to fuck. I didn't mind I busted like 3 nuts. I stayed there and was getting money this went on for months while TJ was on the side eaten. He didn't want no parts of Homestead.

"Tony grab that phone for me." "Yo"

"Is you coming over to the side or what?"

"Naw I'm getting that money bro."

"Man that's all you do, lets hit the club or something."

"Nope paperchasen"

"Man I'll holla at you tomorrow, peace."

"TJ what's up, that nigga still over that broad Tony's house?"

"Shay Shay call Mark and ask him is he trying to hit the club his phone just ringing"

"Yo Mark is this Shay"

"Yo Shay let me see that phone, Mark get dressed this is TJ I'm already on my way."

"Alright"

"We gonna hit club laga"

"Holla when you get here cuz."

"One." "Shay look on the backseat and see if you see that food I'm hungry as fuck."

"Here"

"Good luck cuz"

"You want some of this?"

"What is it TJ?"

"Some ribs and biscuits from the shop in Wilkinsburg."

"Yeah. Good look"

"Yo it be dark as fuck down Hoodtown, don't it Shay. Man I ain't going to keep hitting the horn for this nigga Yo Mark come the fuck on."

"Hold up nigga"

"Okay cuz I see you with the new fits on iced out as usual."

"You know it pimpin"

"Cuz, lock that door and we out."

"Scared ass nigga, ain't nobody trying to carjack you TJ."

"You never know."

"What's up Shay?"

"Chilling homey maintaining,"

"I feel you"

"Look dog it's packed in that bitch, L-Roy coming?"

"Naw he chillen and don't forget to lock the doors"

"Man we got you."

Meanwhile back at my mom's house

"Reida girl what's the matter."

"Victoria it just feels like something going to happen to one of my babies."

"Girl they damn near grown."

"I just miss them now that they're gone all the time."

"Girl just pass the beer I'm trying to get it in while the grandkids are gone."

"Girl I hear you I hear you."

"Just stop worrying."

"Okay only for you"

"Only for me, because you stressing me out, and put Marvin back on you know that's my man and he the only one who could get me out my clothes."

"Well how did you make them other two?'

"It sure wasn't their dad. Marvin was playing and he took my mind somewhere else. Reida put the music on girl."

CHAPTER 5

"Ronnie B I'm tired of that nigga TJ ridin around acting like he's the shit, we get way more money than that bitch ass nigga."

"You gone G thrill, that's them pills man."

"I'm getting tired of everybody saying it's the pills."

"Alright, It ain't the pills man."

"Ronnie B we need to tape that nigga up and take everything he got."

"Man it's up to you G thrill, you know I really don't like them Northside niggas no way, Hill niggas be the wildest"

"Ike call Shady and Rizzi tell them we going to hit the club up because thats where that nigga be at all we gotta do is ride down Bentley and pick them up."

"I think they still at that dice game Thrill."

29

Now everybody know me and them niggas from the Hill didn't get along, not everyone from the hill just Ronnie B, G thrill, Rizzy and that bitch ass nigga Shady. The reason I really don't like shady because he was supposed to be cool but when his niggas came around he was trying to talk to me crazy so I checked him then he snuck me and I still dogged that lame ass nigga. I didn't meet the rest of his click until I went to placement and they told me where they were from and who they were cool with. We just didn't get along and if you didn't get along with me you didn't get along with nobody from Pittsburgh. So we stayed dumpin them niggas and giving them blanket parties. Sometimes by myself, with Ray J, Bay Bay or sometimes Mark. I would ride over to the hill and give them niggas the blues just for GP. So when anybody see me on the hill they just start running

"Sharon bring Shawnese and Shawn Jr. upstairs."

"Mom I'm cooking."

"Sharon bring them upstairs because I'm in the tub and I can't hit them from here."

"Mom hold on please, every time I'm cooking something has to go wrong, SJ and Shawnese come here."

"Girl can you hear me, come on in, I got them from here. Shut the door."

"I hate this shit, Sheena need to come home and take care of her kids and stop partying all the fucking time."

"Sharon grab the wipes from behind the dresser."

"Mom Sheena's right here." "Go see what your mom want and here take these with you hoe."

Sheena had kids by my man Shawn she said he never would come out when he would nut. It was funny to me because Shawn was a funny looking dude but he had change and would get girls drunk, give them x pill then fuck them. I would always clown him but he didn't care because he was getting plenty of pussy and fucking all the young hoes in the hood, all of them.

"Hey Tony let's go out"

"Where you trying to go baby?"

"Let's hit Atlantic City"

"Man that's chump change L-Roy, I got fam down Miami, let's get that body out in the public."

"How much you trying to take down Tony?"

"About 15"

"15 what?"

"Stacks"

"Tone, I only got 20k to myself."

"Don't worry about it baby it's my treat."

"I'm tired of you paying for everything."

"Baby I know you love me and that's all I'm worried about."

31

So as I start packing my clothes I was wondering are we going to drive down or fly but I knew Tony she would want to fly so I didn't even ask.

"L-Roy which outfit you like better?"

Now I knew not to say nothing, I knew she would want to go shopping.

"Never mind L-Roy, we'll hit the store when we get down there."

I just kept my mouth closed

"L-Roy?"

"What's up baby?"

"Did you know I got a little condo down Miami?"

"No but since you said something about it how long you trying to stay down there?"

"About nine months"

"For what?"

"I get money down there too, everywhere I go I'm on."

"I'm cool with it."

"Don't worry L-Roy, if I get money you get money."

"Come here baby and give daddy a kiss." I called a cab to take us to the airport, it was packed like it was a holiday or something but when we finally got on the plane it was

nice. It was my first time flying and once we got in the air I went to sleep, I wanted it to be over as fast as possible. When I woke up we still weren't there yet and Tony was asleep. I looked out the window and all you could see was sky so I just laid back and relaxed my nerves. When we got close, I woke Tony up she looked like some kind of creature or something just waking up talking about she wants a kiss I told her she better go brush your teeth or something she just pushed me away and I started laughing.

"You're going to like my family L-Roy." Tony said as she leaned over to me.

"I wasn't joking right go brush your teeth, your shit banging."

"Only if you hear me out."

"Nope I don't have no ears."

"I'll be right back" She said while walking to the back of the plane.

"Don't rush it."

"Fuck you L, you're mean."

When we landed it was crazy palm trees and shit, hotels on every side of the street and women wearing little to no clothes. So we stopped at this bar for a drink she ordered a pink mojito with some raspberries sticking out of it, it looked on but I stuck to my regular, I shot a belvedere with cranberry and orange juice. We talked about the family she was trying to start with me, I knew

she was drunk because Tony don't do too much talking.

"Do you love me L-Roy?"

"What made you ask me that?"

"Because I'm spilling my guts out and you're not even talking to me"

'Man what's all in that drank because you trippin."

"Do you bae?"

"Yes, Got damn, now leave me alone, come on let's go."

We walked for a while just looking at the sites before finding making our way to her beachfront condo. It was amazing the water was so clear that you could see the fish swimming.

"Look L my peeps are crazy but they gonna like you because you gone too."

"Fuck" I said while reaching in my pocket

"What bae?"

"I aint got my phone, my bro is always looking for me. That's all I got you know."

"No I don't cause I'm here now."

"But."

"But nothing boo I'm a call my uncle."

"What's his name again, Jerry?'

"That's right." "Hello uncle Jerry."

"What's up Tony? It sure took you long enough to come back home, you know we missed you down here."

"Well I'm back for about a year or so."

"That's good, that's real good. You know your mom is in the hospital."

"What's the matter with her now?"

"She caught the flu and couldn't shake it"

"Did they say if she would be okay?"

"You need to go see her and end that beef you have with her, she's still your mother."

"Uncle Jerry what time you coming over?"

"You just don't care do you but expect me around 9 or 10 tonight, okay. Love you."

"Love you too bye."

"L-Roy where you at? You stay in a daze somewhere."

"I was just thinking to myself I always wanted something like this, just to get away you know, if I had the money I would buy my own island."

"Well baby it ain't far, we will get there."

"Did you holla at your people?"

"Yes he said he would be over around 10 tonight."

"Cool, so in the meantime what's for dinner?"

"How about seafood? I know the best spot down here."

"I could go for that, I want lobster, some crab, shrimp, and octopus oh and the biggest clams they got."

"I was thinking the same thing baby but I want a shrimp salad with blue cheese."

"Hold on boo let me call us an order in. It's ringing."

"Hello Salt Water Cafe, how may we help you?"

"Yes Hi I wanted to place a takeout order"

"Yes ma'am what can we get for you?"

"I need 2 shellfish platters, an order of octopus, the biggest claims you have and an order of breaded shrimp. Oh and a shrimp salad with blue cheese."

"Ok ma'am that will be about 30 – 40 minutes"

"Ok thank you."

CHAPTER 6

"Mr. Arthur Gray how are you doing today sir?"

"Just fine before y'all cops came around."

"As you already know I'm Detective Faulk and my partner Detective Jones."

"Man what y'all want"

"Well since you asked. You and I have been doing business for years; you help me solve plenty of cases."

"What is this put my life on front street or something?"

"No Art, let me get right down to the point. Two police officers were killed in the Hill district."

"What does that have to do with me?"

"Well there were no witnesses and no one seems to know anything so I figured let's ask the biggest drug dealer in

western Pennsylvania."

"I seen it on the news but that's about all."

"The streets talk Mr. Gray. So while they're talking and you hear something worthwhile, call me you know the number but if you forgot here's my card."

"Now let's go Mr. Jones we wouldn't want nobody to think Mr. Gray was a snitch. Ain't that right Art."

"I'll contact y'all if I find out anything."

"Thanks again."

"Yeah whatever"

Now Detective Faulk and Jones were homicide detectives and straight dickheadz. Faulk was old white and going through something. Jones was about 6'5 dumb as a brick and Faulk would use him to pound on people most of the time they didn't even have anything on anybody but after getting an ass kicking by Jones you would confess. They were Pittsburgh's Mr. Friendly and they were going to solve a case even if it meant they had to lie but somebody was going to jail

"Bay Bay, Bay Bay"

"What cuz?"

"There go them niggas right there."

"Go grab the k cuz."

"Open the door Shawn, hurry up" while pounding on the

door

"Come in. What the jakes out there or something?"

"Naw them bitch ass niggas who killed Angel."

"Where they at?"

"Over Sheena's house, let me see AK cuz"

"Be careful with my shit Ray J"

"I'm cool, I'm with Bay Bay"

"Fuck DAT don't get my shit fucked up."

"I got you."

"Here this extra clip might come in handy."

"Look Bay Bay I got it. You use that, I got L-Roy's Mac."

"When you get that?"

"Man don't worry about all that, you ready?"

"What you think nigga."

"Let's wait until they come out near they car and shit."

"All right bro."

"Man this niggas taking all day to get slumpt. What time y'all watch got?"

"Man it's only been 15 minutes, shut the fuck up."

"Who you talking to."

"You nigga."

"If you. Here they go."

"Here they go man, get down Ray J. let them get a little closer."

"Man I'll chew them up with the K from here."

"Just be cool."

"Alright I got you."

"Man that bitch gave the best head."

"Man fuck Sheena, what about her thick ass sister, what's her name?"

"Sharon I think"

"Now she's worth spending some money on. I'll trick with her mom too. She thicka then a motha fucka,"

"Throw me the keys to the whip."

"Be cool aint nobody out here."

"I got it."

"Look Ray J you take the one on the right and all take the one on the left."

"For sure,"

"Ready lets rock."

"What's up now playa?"

By the time one knew what was going on Ray J hit him with about 30 shots and his mans ran on him getting it all in the back. He almost got away until he looked down at his chest and seen a big ass hole in his chest and fell right on his face. Bay Bay ran up on him.

"Naw cuz let me get this one."

"Go ahead man but this ain't no game" Ray J let the rest of the rounds go in the back of his head then unzipped his pants and tried to piss on him when Bay Bay pulled him away.

They ran off and headed into the apartment buildings. After that the hood was hot two bodies and no one had seen a thing. Jones and Faulk went on a rampage but this time they had a lead because right in the bushes was a shinny gun wiped off. A Mac 11 that Bay Bay threw to be found like he was taught. They were so happy to find something in usually it would take months for them to get it but this was a double murder and they got the information back the same day and they traced it to the two police officers in the hill district.

"Jones let's take this gun and run it through ballistics."

"Pamela, I need a favor out of you."

"What is it Faulk?"

"Run this through for me."

"It's packed right now, you have to wait."

"Come on Pam. There was a double murder up Northview Heights a few hours ago and they left us a little gift too. Please run it Pam."

"Alright give me about five minutes."

"Thanks I hope we get something this time."

"Don't worry about it Jones some things come together for us, you just have to have faith."

"I have something to tell you fellas. This gun matched up with the shells from the shooting of the two officers in the Hill district."

CHAPTER 7

I remember when I was around five years old my dad was real deep into the whole church thing he knew the Bible inside out my mom did too. When I was born I was baptized and the whole nine. I grew up learning about God and I never thought about the bad things in life even if they were all around me. My mom kept us in the house and I could say I never knew evil and my mom was drug-free and full of life. My dad was a wonderful man 6'3 235 pounds brown skin and well structured. My home was wonderful I would always stay over the Rev's house. Rev. Vaughn was a short fat black guy in his mid 40s. A guy I always thought was cool, he would take us out on field trips like to the zoo, baseball games, we had our own games we would play too like tug-of-war, football, tag, hide and go seek and so much more. One day when I was over Rev. Vaughn's pool he jumped in as usual.

"Rev the water is cold."

"Yes Leroy it is."

"Where is everyone else at Rev?"

"At home. I told him it's just me and you today."

So Rev. Von was trying to pull my pants down and I was trying to get away. I thought he was playing but he really had something else on his mind. I never paid it no mind but when he grabbed my butt I asked him what he was doing and he said he was just playing.

A few days later another thing happened when I was using the bathroom he walked in on me while I was taking a dump and I told him to leave but he wouldn't he just stood there looking at me then he just went away. One day after a meal I felt real sleepy I didn't know why but later I had found out that Rev Vaughn put some type a sleeping pill in my juice and I was out cold. What had happened is while I was asleep Rev Vaughn raped me but I never woke up. While all this was happening my dad was calling the house trying to get the Rev on the phone but he had turned it off so my dad decided to pop up.

"Reida baby, I don't know what's going on over there but I'm a ride over."

"Baby he's fine, he's just not around the phone at this time."

"Well it won't hurt for me to ride over."

"Okay, I'll be upstairs when you get back."

As the door closes. "Where are my keys, there they go."

The church was located down on California Avenue so it only took about 5 to 10 minutes from Northview. "Any other day the traffic would be fine but when I'm trying to get somewhere its jam packed. All the lights are on, I'll park right here."

When my dad gets out the car and walks up the steps he keeps hearing a noise but he paid it no mind. He gets to the door and rings the bell. ding dong ding dong. Inside Rev Vaughn and has the music on loud so he doesn't hear the door bell.

"What is that noise?" He said when he heard noises that sounded like someone moaning.

"Let me go to the back." He climbs over the fence then hits the ground.

"That looks like them. I wonder why they ain't get the door."

He only saw a shadow so he didn't know what was going on.

"Man it look like this backdoors cracked let me go on in."

Now on his way up the steps the moaning noise is getting louder not even paying attention to the music playing. Now my dad's at the top of the steps and sees something he never thought he would see in this lifetime a grown man on top of his firstborn child raping him while he's asleep. He dug in his pocket and found a pen he rushed towards the Rev.

"Man what the fuck are you doing?" While pulling him off me and stabbing him with the pen. The Rev never had a chance, my dad was too strong. By the time the police got there they said you couldn't even tell who the Rev was and my dad was still screaming how could you. So when my dad didn't come back right away, my mom took a little ride of her own down to the house. When she finally made it upstairs my dad was so gone my mom just called the police. My dad got life, I don't see him or nothing. Every time I think about it more hate brews inside of me and I have to think about a man raping me. That's why my mind is so fucked up now and I'll never be the same. My mom broke down and she start smoking crack now my family is in the ruts because of one man. He was supposed to deliver us from evil not bring us into destruction.

"Yo Rizz."

"Shady what's the deal Ike?"

"Look here hold up Ike I'm up 10 stacks."

"Shady you ain't doing nothing Ike."

"You know I gotta watch this nigga Ike he's crazy."

"Thrill just pull over Ike fuck that I'm robbin these niggas Ike."

"What about Shady and Rizz?"

"They better move Ike."

"Come on hold up Ike."

Before Ron B could even get out the car you heard the pump get cocked.

"Everybody get on the fucking ground."

"Thrill what you doing Ike?"

"Get the fuck out of my face Ike before y'all niggas be next. Go get in the car or something grab the rest of that money up Shady and come on."

"Ronnie B check them niggas for guns Ike."

"They cool G."

"Everybody strip and hurry the fuck up. Bitch you better hurry up."

"But I ain't got nothing on under this."

"Bitch you think I'm playing." As G Thrill takes the butt of the shotty and cracks her across the face with it. "You still ain't got nothing on?"

"Okay okay."

"I want everything besides clothes put in front of you. Ronnie B handle that, there go a bag over there hurry up nigga."

"I'm done thrill."

"And thank you for your support."

"Come on thrill let's be out."

"I can't find the keys."

"They right there on the floor Ike." Shots start hitting the car.

"Man somebody's busting on us."

"Fuck, let me see that." G Thrill gets back out the car and is letting loose with the ruger. Shadys like fuck that nigga and jumped in the driver seat and pulled off on thrill leaving him. When Thrill's gun emptied, he turned around to try to get back in the car as they were already pulling off with. Shady screaming "fuck you, you broke ass nigga". G Thrill tried to run but was gunned down on his last breath he was trying to talk. "Please don't kill me." That same female he hit across the face told him "What you thought it was a game Ike" and ended G thrills life.

CHAPTER 8

"What's up baby?"

"Don't call me baby, you don't know me nigga."

"Fuck you then bitch."

"Fuck you, you little skinny ass nigga."

"Mark be cool cuz."

"I'm sorry baby girl."

"That's alright TJ, you just better let your friend know watch how he talk to people."

"Man move, talk to this bitch." Mark moved TJ and spit all in her face and pushed her to the ground. "Get the fuck out of my face trick and watch who you talking to." She stormed off scraped up and embarrassed.

"Mark you drunk or something man?"

"Shay you know I'm feeling it but she came at me first."

"Fuck it let's hit the dance floor cuz. Where TJ go?"

"I don't know he around here somewhere."

"Hi Shay, Hi Mark."

"Tammy who's your friend?"

"Mark, Shay this is Meeka."

"Where you from baby doll?"

"Manchester."

"Okay, okay Northside in the house!"

"You're from the side too?"

"Of course, I'm from Hoodtown." "and I'm from the Heights."

"Y'all trying to dance?"

"We ain't doing no trying, we going to burn y'all."

"TJ baby you still got them pills?"

"I need 20 a pill player."

"Come on TJ we better than that, I got 15 bucks for you."

"Here, but I still want my five bucks."

"Good look TJ, I think that your phone ringing."

"Oh good look. Hello?"

"What's up?"

"Who's this?"

"Toya"

"What's up?"

"I need a half bottle of them joints."

"I'm a need 600."

"Where you at?"

"Club laga"

"I'll be there in about 10 minutes, be outside TJ I'm not trying to come in."

"I got you."

"Mark let me see the dro."

"Man where you been at?"

"Making money hoe, you know. Hurry up cuz, I got this sale coming man. Good look."

"Where you going now man?"

"I'll be back." TJ says while walking back outside.

"Ronnie B start counting that cash Ike."

"Come on Ike I'm already on top of that."

"When you're done we going to drop that off at the spot and look for them niggas."

"Yo Ike everybody at club laga Ike. Hoes get in for free and the first hundred get drinks free."

"That's what I'm talking about Ike."

"The guns in the trunk."

"Alright let's step to the next level Ike."

"Hey shady."

"What's up?"

"We hit for about 36 stacks, 2 zones, 5 watches, a diamond bracelet, 4 chains and 6 rings."

"Here let me see that bag, we'll split this shit up later. I'll be right back."

"Look y'all, I ain't just tryna slump em Ike, we need some of that cash he got Ike."

"I feel you Rizzy, we could duct tape that nigga Ike put him in the trunk or something."

"I got you Ike wait till shady come back."

"Come on y'all ready."

"Look shady we ain't gonna slump that nigga right away."

"I know Ike we going to hit him for that change Ike."

"Damn Ike club Laga packed."

"Make sure you park close Ike so when we drag that nigga out Ike."

"Y'all ready?"

"Stop playing Ike, let's trunk this nigga and be out."

"Look Ike."

"What Rizzi?"

"That's that nigga right there with that bitch."

"Ain't that something. Rizzi walk right up on him because he really don't know you. Me and Ron B got him from the side."

"Yo what's up Ike?"

"Who you fam?" TJ replies

"You don't remember me?"

"Look fam I aint got time for games, I'm out."

"Nigga don't turn your back on me." Crack to the back of the head TJ gets hit with the gun.

"Shit what the fuck you doing?"

"What's up TJ?"

"Fuck you Shady!"

"Naw Ike you coming with us."

"Man get the fuck off me."

"Pull that nigga leg off and choke him out Rizzy."

"Come on put him in the backseat nigga, start the car up let's get the fuck out of here."

"We finally got one of these niggas Ike."

"I really want that nigga L-Roy, he always on the hill bussin his gun Ike."

"We gonna get him too Ike, just fall back."

"Hurry up Ronnie B."

"What you want to get pulled over something?"

"Naw be cool then Shady, we all most there."

As they approach, Rizzy is getting nervous and has to open the window to get some air. They pull up in front of the house Shady is the first one to grab him and pull him out the car. Rizzy helps grab him and Ronnie B follows them up the steps and into the house.

"Grab the duct tape from under the desk. Ya'll put him in the chair here, leave his mouth open and wrap up the rest of him."

Shady smacks TJ right across the face "Wake your bitch ass up" he smacks him again "Wake up."

"Throw some cold water on him."

"Hold up Ike let me grab some."

"Yo Ike we gotta go to that niggas stash and get that nigga to come up with someone to call."

"Someone?"

"That nigga Art."

"No doubt Ike no doubt."

"Look out Ike." Splash water is thrown in his face.

"Hey what's up homie, I see you woke now, now you know what I want so just give it to me and I might let you go."

"Alright look if you suck my dick bitch I might give you a dollar."

"I like that TJ." Shady says while laughing

"Suck my dick shady."

"I like that, I knew you were going to say something real fly."

"You're going to kill me anyway, so fuck you all."

"Nope not that simple TJ, not today, I want you to meet my little friend." Shady whispers "go get that little handheld saw from the basement Ronnie B" then he turns to TJ "and you, I like you Ike, so look, I'm a give you another chance before I get nasty."

"Alright shady, come a little closer so I could talk to you."

"What man, you must think this is some movie or

something."

"Naw I'm serious, I just don't want everybody to know."

"Them my niggas, they gonna know regardless, but look I see you tryna work with me, so what is it?"

As Shady moves towards TJ with his head down, TJ musters up out loogie from down below and puts it between Shadys eyes. Shady snaps runs up to Ronnie B grabs the saw and goes straight to TJ.

"So you want to play you little bitch?"

"Pick that nigga up and turn him around and put his fingers on the table." Shady says to Ronnie B while TJ tries to get loose.

"Rough him up some and hold him down."

As soon Shady put the saw to his fingers he screams "Alright I'll tell you where the money at.

"Hold that thought." while Shadys cutting one of his fingers off everybody's looking dazed, they never did nothing like this before. Now is the finger comes off Shady shows it to TJ. "Now where you say that shits at?"

TJ starts to cry thinking he's going to die.

"Oh don't worry you ain't going to die" "Pick him up and take him to the stove."

While picking him up, they see that the blood is squirting out crazy. They make it over to the stove but it's

an electric stove so they have to wait until it heats up.

"I'll tell you where the shit at I promise."

"Don't worry I got you." "Put his finger on there it will stop the bleeding."

"Please stop I'll tell you."

"I know you will but this will stop the bleeding."

"Go ahead." Shady motions for them to put his finger on the stove.

"No no please don't." As they put his finger on the heat he goes crazy. "Shit, fuck, fuck please just kill"

"Alright that's cool." "I'm going to make sure you don't die on me."

"I told you before I will tell you where the money is at."

"But you were playing around homie, now where the safe at?"

"It's at my mom's crib."

"What's the combo?"

"27 right 36 left and 10 right, please don't hurt my mother, please."

"Come on man, I'm not heartless. What all in there TJ?"

"About 97 stacks 2 keys, a glock, 2 pounds of weed, 9 oz of heroin and 10 bottles of X pills."

"Damn you eaten youngin!"

"Please just don't kill my mom that's all I have." While tears come down TJ's eyes he knew he was done.

"You cool, don't worry." "Now TJ I need one more thing maybe two. Give me your uncle Art's number and your x pill connect."

"Look 412-555-1212 that's my uncle Art's number and 412-555-5555 that's fat rat's number for the X pills. Please don't kill him."

"Who fat rat?"

"Naw my uncle."

"I got you."

"Look first we gonna head over his moms crib, what's the address?"

"637 Chicago St"

"Then call fat rat and then Art."

"Well somebody has to stay here with him."

"You stay Rizzy and me and Ronnie B a go Ike."

"I'm cool with that."

"Let's roll"

On the way out Shady tells Ronnie be about killing all three of them. Ronnie B just starts laughing. The drive to

the Northside things are very quiet, with Ronnie B thinking about where he's going to move to after he gets the money and Shady thinking to himself how he's going to run the hill one day. They pull up and see there's no one out, it's a gloomy night with a light drizzle. As they get out the car and start to knock on the door Shady tells Ronnie B to hold up and calls the spot and find to where the safe is. Rizzi picks up the first ring. "What's up Ike?"

"Ask TJ where the safe is."

"Where the safe Ike?"

"Under my bed, he'll see a small rug, it's under that."

"Did you hear him?"

"I got it Ike."

They knock on the door guns at hand, no masks on as soon as Ms Reida opens the door she gets bum rushed and choked out. "Make sure aint nobody else in the house Ronnie B." Shady says.

"I got you."

As he smacks Reida, she wakes up. "U a fine ass bitch ain't you."

"What y'all want, aint nobody here."

"But you are."

"Please don't hurt me."

"Don't worry about it, it won't hurt."

"Please no."

"Shut up bitch and get on your stomach." As he pulls down his pants he calls the spot and tells Rizzi put TJ on the phone.

"What's up man?"

"Here, say hi."

"Hello, baby give them what they want."

"Mom what are they doing?"

"He's…" As shady pulls his dick out, he pulls her pants down and rips her panties off. She begins to cry but doesn't struggle. Shady tells her just take it like a woman.

"Mom what's happening?"

"Nothing baby just give them what they want."

"Don't move or I'll kill you bitch." Shady whispers in her ear while forcefully entering her asshole. Stroke after stroke she cries more and more asking why. He tells her to shut up and then hangs the phone up asking her if she liked it calling her a nasty bitch. He was in it longer than she thought and she was starting to climax and was pumping back. Shady had a little more than what she usually had and she kind of liked it. It's been years but she wouldn't tell him.

After he collected everything, Ronnie B slides in for a sneak peek. Shady told him to come on and she's wide-open so Ronnie B jumped on in and joined. Shady was

putting her on all fours but still in her asshole while Ronnie B unzipped his pants and put it in her mouth going down deep, thrusting deep in her mouth she gagged and threw up from his manhood. As they switched Reida was a little nervous because Ronnie B was going in her ass too and she couldn't take no more she tried to put her hands back there but Ronnie B just pushed them away and he continued to pound on it. She started moaning and screaming telling him to stop but he didn't, he just went harder and harder until her asshole started to bleed and shady got up and took a picture with his phone to show everyone.

While Ronnie B is pounding her asshole he feels he's about to nut so he grabs her hair and starts spanking her on her ass like if he were riding her then he came inside her and pushed her to the ground. Shady asked again if she liked it, she knew he was for real, so she said they were good all the time saying to herself this man is insane. Then the unexpected happened Shady pulls out his gun and shot her several times killing her on the spot. Ronnie B ran to the car and got some gas and put it all over the house, Shady pulled out his lighter fired up a blunt and set the whole place on fire then they were out. Back at the spot Rizzy was talking to TJ telling him how easy it would've went. "All you had to do Ike is tell us where the shit was and he probably would've been gone by now." TJ just sat there not saying a word. He had that thought in his head that deep feeling about his mother being gone.

Ronnie B and Shady start to call fat rat. "Hello who is this?"

"Who is this nigga, you called my phone."

"My bad homie this is Matt, TJ's man."

"What's the deal baby?"

"TJ said he need 10 more bottles."

"Alright give me about 10 minutes and meet me on Boyle Street near Federal Street."

"Rat yo what color car you going to be in?"

"All black caddy truck."

"Alright homey, one." "Let's go down there and set up before that nigga come." They went down on Boyle and posted up.

"Yo you stay in the car Ike."

"Where you going shady?"

"I'm a post up in the cut so when that nigga pull up Ike I could see who's with him."

"Cool."

"Be ready Ike."

"Aint I always."

Shady walks around the block acting like he's looking for fiends for a ride or something a couple minutes later fat rat pulls up. Shady calls Ronnie B on his cell "Yo Ike that's that nigga right there, get ready Ike."

"Man I got this."

"After I look in, I'll give you the signal to walk up to fat rat."

"I got you."

As Shady walks passed the truck still on the phone with Ronnie B, he spots 2 guys with fat rat and tells Ronnie B to approach slowly to give him enough time to get back around the corner. While he was looking in one of fat rats men spot him peeking. "Rat"

"What's cracking?"

"That nigga all looking in cuz."

"Fuck that nigga he probably just hating."

Now Shady's peeking around the corner looking at the ride and he tells Ronnie B go ahead but walk slow. Now when Ronnie B taps on the window for rat Shady's almost there. "You TJ's man?" Rat asks. While he's talking shady begins to fire hitting the guy in the front seat with numerous shots and hitting the guy in the backseat. While fat rat tries to pull out his gat, Ronnie B catches him with one in his shoulder blade making him drop his weapon and sending shots to the back hitting Ronnie B too. Shady opens the door and pulls both lifeless bodies out of the car and is going over to the other side pushing fat rat to the passenger seat seeing his man's bleeding. "You good b?"

"Naw that bitch ass nigga got me in the chest."

"Fuck b get in the other car and follow me, hurry up cuz

you know the Jakes coming." They head straight downtown and then back to the hill right to the spot. As they are walking to the door Shady says to Rat "Get your fat ass up this bitch before I put something in you to make you lose weight." Ronnie B passes out. "Fuck Ike, Rizzy Rizzy." he screams for him to come out.

"Ike what the fuck?"

"He was hit Ike. Take him in the house, I got rat ass." Rizzy gets him in the house, he knows he's dead and begins to wig out taking it out on Rat.

"Be cool Ike that ain't going to bring Ronnie B back Ike."

"Fuck that where the money at Ike?"

"I'll call and get…" In the middle of the sentence Rizzy pulls out his gun in smacks fat rat across the face with it.

"Man I just reed up I aint got no money."

Bang! Rizzi bangs him in the leg. "Where the money bitch, the next one a be in ya head, nigga."

"Calm down Ike we need him alive."

"You calm down Ike nobody said nothing when you cut that niggas finger off when he spit all in your face Ike. So let me do me Ike."

"Alright when he die you did you."

"I really want to kill him anyway." Rizzy says to Shady.

"Ike go ahead, I don't give a fuck we up." Before fat rat

could talk Rizzy just start shooting him.

"TJ call that nigga Art." "Take the tape off that fools hands and hurry up."

TJ just kept his comments to himself. The phone starts and when uncle Art picked up TJ hung up. "I guess he ain't home."

"Let me see that, it's ringing here."

"Who's this?"

"Uncle Art it's TJ."

"What's up boy. Where you at? Mark and your other little friend came passed here looking for you they said you dipped on them while y'all was at the club.

Shady is whispering for TJ to tell Art to meet him somewhere.

"That wasn't about nothing, I was just caught up but look I need to holla at you in person."

"What's the matter Neff?"

"Just holler at me."

"Alright meet me at the spot."

"Naw I can't meet you in front of the police station."

"Why not that's where we always meet."

"Man fuck all that give me the phone." Shady says while

snatching the phone. "Look nigga we want the cash or it's his ass."

"I ain't got it. I aint got no money."

"You rather hold on to that cash then your blood?" "Here TJ beg him for your life."

"Uncle Art if I didn't have to ask you I wouldn't."

"But Neff I aint got it, not even no work, nope nothing."

"They cut off one of my fingers."

"I ain't got it."

"But you on more than me."

"Bye Neff." Art says while hanging up the phone.

"He hung up on me." TJ tells Shady.

"Don't worry TJ he dead and you're dead too. But that was cold."

They began duct taping TJ placing him in the deep freezer, turning it up on high, locking him in it then they left.

CHAPTER 9

"Mom guess what happen?" Sheena says to Ms Victoria

"What girl spit it out."

"Ms. Reida's house caught on fire last night and they said they found her body in there."

"Are they sure it's her?"

"No but that's who the police think it is."

"Okay Sheena call up TJ."

"He's not picking up, neither is L-Roy. I haven't seen TJ in about three days and I haven't seen L-R-Roy in about five months."

"Did your sister see any of them?"

"Nope she was trying to."

"What about their cousin Mark?"

"I don't know his number mom."

"Well baby all we can do is pray and hope they're okay because all Reida was talking about is her babies."

"Me too mom, I hope they are okay."

"So Mr. L-Roy are you ready to eat?"

"Of course I am!"

"Well I'll be right back."

"Baby girl give me a kiss goodbye."

"Okay only if you sing to me."

As I begin to sing she kisses all me all tongue action then runs out the door. While she's gone I'm thinking about my family but I know they're okay. What I'll do is lay low down here for a year and chill make them think about me then move everyone out the hood.

"L-Roy don't you hear me calling you?"

"Naw what's up?"

"Come and help me with this food and we left all them bags we brought outside."

"My bad girl, I'm coming."

I went downstairs then we sat down together and started to eat. Sitting there I started daydreaming about

everything I could be doing if I got rich. While Tony is talking to me I really can't hear her because I'm deep in thought and I only could see her mouth moving. By the time I got done thinking she was mumbling something about her uncle and how much money he had. After dinner we laid on the bed and watch movies until her uncle showed up. Now when I heard the doorbell I got up and got dressed and Tony went down to open the door. When I saw him it shocked me because he was a very short man, balding on top and he looked like he was mixed with something. I would later find out he was half Chinese so was Tony. We never talked about any business but he asked me would I like to visit his home one day. I told him I don't care and he told me to pack up. So I did just that and he told Tony we'll be back in about a month. I didn't say anything or ask any questions. On the ride to his home we talked a lot about Tony and he said she must trust me a lot because she don't even trust her own mother and if my baby trust you so do I. So we pull up to the small condo he told me to wait there then he came back out with a small bag I didn't ask him what it was because I didn't care.

"So where are you from L-Roy?"

"Pittsburgh"

"I've been there before. Tell me where you getting money in Pittsburgh?"

"I still am."

"Okay how much work do you think you could handle?"

"I don't know something major."

"Well we are going to find out."

We were on the road for a while before I passed out like I always did. When I woke up, the sun was up and we were still on the road. I seen a sign that said welcome to Mississippi and I said to myself it's on baby. I think it said Jackson or something we wasn't there that long. Not even long enough for me to even take a piss for real and when I did I was rushed and this was at some rundown apartments. When I was on my way out the door he threw me a big black plastic bag and it was heavy then we switched cars and got in this big van. When we were inside he hit some buttons on the door then the floor started coming up. I just watched then he finally talked. "Put that bag in there." Then we were off again. I wanted to ask him where we were going but I didn't I just leaned back in my seat and grabbed my headphones and went in a zone. Music does that to me.

We stopped for gas at a few places but I never looked up, I didn't want to see no police. When we stopped again he was telling me get the drugs from below me. I had to say something so I asked him where we were at.

"South Carolina" He said.

"What part?"

"Columbia"

"I heard of it but I never been there before."

Where we parked at was crazy in the cut. We went through these paths then we finally came to a house that

was real old looking with a lot of land around it. There were chickens and dogs were running around and some old man was sitting on the porch with a pipe in his hand talking to himself. We just walked passed him went in the house. Uncle Jerry talked to some old lady then she looked at me and just smiled and finish talking. I got tired of standing there so I sat down on the couch.

No one was talking me so I zoned out thinking about my future and how much money I was going to stack. By the time I came out of my zone it was nighttime and Jerry was coming down the steps. I said goodbye to the old lady and we were out. Now on the road everything was pretty quiet so I turned my music on and as soon as it came on Jerry took the headphones off of me and started talking.

"So L-Roy you ready?"

"Ready for what?"

"To get this money. We're on our way to the ATL and it moves fast."

"Man I was born ready."

"Look I got 40 keys in the floor and another 60 bricks in the front panel."

My mouth dropped and I couldn't believe we were riding with 100 bricks.

"L-Roy when we get there we're going to stop at one of the little hoes spot but don't get out stay in the car ducked off. I don't want no one to know you were here."

As soon as we pulled up into the projects, I just sat there while Jerry ran around. By the time he came back to the car it was nighttime and I was starving.

"Look Jerry I'm hungry."

"Just hold up I got an apartment on the Eastside."

So we drove and I looked out the window daydreaming about this money then we pulled up in front of this apartment building.

"That's it right there, I own the whole thing but I let my young hoes keep up with it and just send me 50% of the money. See L-Roy when you take care of these hoes they take care of you."

I just kept quiet. As we got out of the car and went in it was alright though nothing major. The furniture was all leather with marble floors with some good looking women that was half naked. One was named Shaw Shaw. She was kind of chubby with a pretty face but a thick chubby, tan skin, blonde hair, jet black eyes, a small waist and a booty that said please just tear me up. Her lips looked like they just wanted to talk to your dick and she had small breast with big ass nipples.

"Shaw Shaw, this L-Roy." "L-Roy, this Shaw Shaw."

"How you doing L-Roy?"

"What's up?"

I think she was Cambodian or something because she did not speak good English.

"Shaw Shaw watch my cuz for me I'll be back in a couple of hours."

"Okay."

"Where you going Jerry?" I said

"L-Roy you said you were hungry eat and I'll be back in a few."

"So where are you from L-Roy?"

"Miami"

"How old are you?"

"32" I lied, I don't know this chick.

"Look Shaw I'm hungry."

"I'll make you some chicken and macaroni and cheese."

"Good look" as I watched Shaw cook I was getting horny watching her behind. I ate until I was full and I watched TV on the couch hoping Shaw would just come and eat me up all crazy. She came in and sat next to me on the couch not saying a word. Some comedy show was on with some actors I've never seen before.

"L-Roy do you like old karate flicks?"

"Of course I do, who don't."

When she got up to go over to the DVD player, I was thinking about what I could do with all that ass. Then I remembered I had about a half of ounce of some purple in

my shoe and like 10 x pills, that I'll make the mood right.

I pulled out that sticky and waved it in her face and she said "yes I smoke and I got some strawberry wraps, what you know about that young buck".

"Grab something to drink too while you at it Shaw."

She came back with a box of wraps and a bottle of Remy but while she was gone I was crushing up like five pills to put in her drink. I knew she would be gone, they were double stacks too. She got up to use the bathroom I slipped them right in and mix that shit up and it dissolved. When she came back I was still wrapping and shit. We started smoking and got high as hell from the purple and that Remy. I could tell she was buzzing off that pill because she just went in a zone for about 10 minutes. I tapped her to ask her something and she just started shaking it was crazy but I knew it was on so I started whispering in her ear. She started tweaking for the dick and grabbing my shirt. I told her she couldn't give good head so stop playing with my shit. She looked at me like I was crazy then it was on. She was like a pit locked onto my dick and she wouldn't stop. I nutted like three times and I was fingering her asshole the whole time. I don't know what made me do it but I ate her asshole. She started going crazy and I did that for about 20 minutes before I started fucking her in her ass with everything I got. Watching sweat drip down her back and down to her ass made me hornier. When it was all done and over with she was still licking and sucking on my balls with her eyes wide open. I finally dozed off and when I woke up Jerry was back hittin something right in the floor in front of me looking like an

old ass dog humping a leg or something. I got up to wash my face and went to the kitchen to find something to eat. When I opened the refrigerator I was in shock, there was so much food. I started with the basics and worked my way up, eggs, cheese, bacon, hash browns, french toast and some breakfast pastries. I found some ham and threw it with the eggs and I poured myself a glass of orange juice. I was in the kitchen for a long time and when I finally came out I damn near had a heart attack from shock. On the living room floor, was more dope than I've ever seen in my life, pills, weed and guns. I said to myself this man is crazy. So now I'm getting a little paranoid, I looked out the window and seen a big moving truck.

"What are you doing L-Roy?"

"Man Jerry you scared the fuck out of me. Man what are you doing with all this shit in the house?"

"Don't worry this spot ain't hot L-Roy. Anyway this shit will be gone soon and I'll show you what real money looks like. Them fools riding around with their music blasting and gold chains on aint got shit."

"But Jerry there's a lot of shit to get rid of."

"Hold on L-Roy, that's my phone." "Hello yeah come through." Then he turns to me and starts talking again. "Alright look that is like 500,000 right there for five keys of pure dope that could be stepped on about five times and still be deadly."

"So this is all dope?"

"Yup besides that shit in the van."

"Damn" I said in shock

"Now look L-Roy I'm about to give you some clients. Take this cell phone, it's a Nextel so I could just hit you with the direct connect. Here's the number and don't talk business on the phone we do codes I'll show you. Now the dude coming to cop from us his name is Twan. He got money but not like you're going to get money. Feel me?"

"Yeah no doubt Jerry."

"I'm a give you 10 people to work with you could find the rest on your own. I want 50,000 on each key. Now that's cheap because you could step on it twice. Deal?"

"Deal"

"Okay let's get to work and don't worry about the other shit that was so so."

The day went on and we got money. He explained the codes, what he usually wants what, how much the usually spend. The first 10 people came to cop off me and another 10 people for the weed, then more for the guns, pills and coke. I ended up with 50 customers in less than five hours. That's crazy and they spend big money. I sold 500 pounds of Colombian Gold to one of my hits, 30 AKs to another, 60 bricks of coke to another, 10 jars of X pills not little bottles the big protein bottle jars at 15k a pop, 10 bricks of dope at one time that's $1 million for that right there. I had to ask Jerry how much does he think he's worth and he told me around 70 million because he spends a lot of

money. That's crazy he doesn't look like he's worth that. He doesn't dress like it, spend money all like that or even act like it. He told me he has a lot of money wrapped up in land, businesses, homes and investments stuff that no one notices. If I wasn't counting all this cash right now I wouldn't believe it myself.

In one day we were sold out. Dudes was coming from all over the state to cop from Jerry. I thought the big man goes unseen but he's one of the biggest and the people talk to him directly. We counted up around 10 million and 2 million in coke, 500,000 in guns, 300,000 in pills and 100,000 in weed, that's $12,900,000 in one day. That took three days to count and another two days to recount making it five days total. I came out of the deal with 3.5 million for one day when in fact he only had to give me around 2 million. It's not even hard work and I have 50 dudes on my cell who blowing me up and a connect who could give me multiple life sentences any time. All that but I have a family at home who won't answer the phone when I call. I'm rich and it don't even feel like it.

Now Uncle Jerry explains this to me your hits come wherever you're at because the prices are unbelievable. They are hundred thousand for a brick of dope which turns into five bricks of still dope dead, 10,000 for key of pure coke that stepped on and turn into three still bomb coke. 1500 for a pound of Colombian gold, AK-47s for 700 apiece, x pills for two dollars a pill. That's unreal and so much more shit. Now we then left Shaw Shaw's house and went to the mall but not to buy anything but to meet Jerry's connect. He was an old man and wore no jewelry and had a few bodyguards. Come to find out later on Jerry

was the man and he was just using the old man as the front but the old man never knew it. Jerry never bought nothing but was actually growing it pressing it and pricing it but you would never know that my new uncle was not just a drug lord but was the drug lord from China and had billions of dollars. And what he showed me the day before was just a front set up beforehand for them people to buy what they was going to buy. The real deals were going on right next-door he just wanted to see if I was going to steal or do something crazy but I passed the test. Now I'm supplying the whole East Coast with work and most of the southern states. I'm high on the totem pole and don't even know it. I'm making anywhere from 20 to 70 million a week easy and I watch Jerry so much I acted like him. I don't floss at all and I drive a pickup truck. I bought real estate all over the place, got the laundry spot together with my vending machines in it. Me and Tony are still getting money and the deeper me and Tony's relationship got I realize that she had plenty of money that she was not putting out there but I really wasn't worried about it. I went home sick from time to time but I know I have a few months left before I go home. They're going to be so surprised. My mom is going to be crying and all that other stuff when I tell her to pack her things and TJ I could see his face now when I tell him home much I'm worth.

"L-Roy, L-Roy!"

"Yo what's up baby?"

"You always in the zone boy."

"Tony stop it, I'm not trying to hear any of this right

now."

"Well your phones ringing bighead."

"Oh damn." "hello?"

"Yo this J Rizza."

"I think you got the wrong number dog."

"This Jerry."

"Oh what's up, where you at?"

"Up front."

"I'm on my way down." "Tony, I'm out that's Jerry."

"Well could I get a kiss before you go baby, my big businessman."

"When I get back."

"L-Roy come here."

"Holla" I say as I close the door.

Tony mumbles, "I can't stand him."

"Yo what's on the list for the day?"

"Get in, look L-Roy I need you to do me a favor."

"What you need Jerry?"

"Some guy, well some old friend is coming to see me about some business and the word on the street is he's

working with them people. I need you to make sure he never gets to say anything about me."

"When and where?"

"Damn you said you aint do this before."

"Naw but you showed me so much love that I would do anything for you that's all."

"I was hoping you would be ready for this because in this business there will be a lot of this. Look under the seat you'll find a bag. That's a glock 40 with two clips, gloves and a mask. The address of the guy, his name and phone number and the time he goes to work and the time he usually be in the hotel. Just holla at me when it's over. The address is on this side of Miami. I know you don't know your way around all like that but you'll be fine."

"I got you."

"Love you boy like you was one of my own."

"Thanks Jerry for everything."

After I chilled in the house and watched Tony sleeping I finally looked in the bag. I looked at the gun for the safety and checked the clips then wiped it down again. When I was looking at the address at first I was like where the fuck is this and then I remembered. But the biggest shock was the person I had hit was a woman. I'm like damn Jerry that's probably why he said this seems to be real easy for me. A woman I got it but fuck it, makes me think about Angel and how she died but business is

business and Jerry says it's got to be done so it's done. As night falls in I get dressed in them convenient color robbers and other thugs in hoods love to wear when they're about to put in work. I say to myself there is no turning back now not because this was my first time but this woman never did anything to me. I had to say a prayer for her so I did and I was out. I kissed Tony on her big forehead because she was still sleeping. I looked at the time on the list

Jerry gave me it said she would be home around 10 but I wanted to be there way before to make sure everything went smooth. Now the only thing I didn't understand is why Jerry never gave me a picture of her so now I had to ask. I walked into the hotel lobby; I went straight to the steps and right to the janitor. I took the key to her room, tied him up, put him in the bathroom. I waited in her room so when the door opened I was behind it and before she could shut it; the gun was already to her head. But there was something I did not expect to happen a little boy walked in right behind her it caught me off guard but he still didn't see me so I told her tell him to go into the bathroom. "Man Man go into the bathroom." He looked at me I was just like damn but I did not let him see the gun. He looked like he was around seven or eight years old so he would've known what it was.

I asked her for her name.

"Regina Taylor."

"And your nickname is our RT?"

"Yeah, why?"

Now I thought about little dude in the bathroom and him not having his mother so I asked her "Is that your son?"

"Yes that is my baby."

"How old is?"

"He's six years old."

"Look ma'am I don't have nothing against your son and I promise he will be taken care of."

"What are you talking about?" She replied.

So I asked her did she know Jerry she said yes. I asked her what did he look like, I had to be sure. This was not easy for me especially with the baby there. She said short caramel hair, balding in the front. That was enough. I did it, I pulled the trigger not once but the whole clip, I had to make sure no slipups. I took off down the hallway and went into the janitor's closet and put the gun in there with the clothes and set them on fire. I ran down the back steps without anyone noticing me. There were a whole bunch of people just standing around like nothing happened; I guess they did not hear the gunshots. That's not my problem anymore; I got a cab to get back home. It was only a couple blocks away from the house but I did not feel like walking. My mind was still thinking about what I've done and the child. When I got back Tony was in the shower and some R Kelly was playing on the stereo, I took my clothes off when I heard the water in the bathroom stop running and sat on the bed. I know Tony was probably horny and I have been ducking that ass for some time. When she stepped out the bathroom she had

her birthday suit on and I just smiled.

"Baby before you do or say anything I want to tell you I love you."

"Oh L-Roy I love you too."

"So tonight baby we are going to make love."

"Why you say it like that bae? We always make love."

"No we don't baby, me pounding on it and nutting all over you is not making love. I want to take my time and please you like you need to be pleased."

"You always please me L-Roy."

"Look Tony just be cool and enjoy this baby."

She just was quiet and smiled. We made love all night but in the back of my head was the lady and her son. Damn life is crazy but I got to get this money. When I woke up in the morning I was shocked, Tony was up and watching the news with a nice breakfast made. She told me mine was sitting in the warmer then I grabbed her and pulled her up close to me. She shocked me again.

"L-Roy your food is right there."

"I see it babe."

"Are you okay L-Roy?"

"Why you say that?"

"Because uncle Jerry told me what happened last night."

"What are you talking about?"

"The hit. I know everything you and my uncle do."

"Look girl, I don't know what you're talking about and I don't know why Uncle Jerry be telling you what we do."

"Look bae I brought you into this because I knew you could handle it."

"I still don't know what you're talking about."

"L-Roy the news is on in and that part is about to come on about some lady getting killed in a hotel."

"Oh yeah?"

When it came on I was so angry because Jerry already told her what happened. They were showing the little boy and I felt so sad for him because he was still crying and it made me think about my family. I know once this year was up I would be so happy to see my family.

CHAPTER 10

As time went on in Miami, I just stacked every day and I lived in fear that I would be set up or killed out here on the streets. I've been lucky the closest thing is when this dumbass cop pulled me over. I know I didn't have no license so I don't ride real dirty. I mean as long as I can hide it and they can't find it. This dude had to be a nut.

"License and registration please."

"I don't have no license but I have insurance."

"Please get out of the car and place your hands on the hood. Do you have any weapons or drugs on you?"

"No sir."

As he pats me down it brought back memories of me splitting them pigs when I was younger. Now I try to stay away from that type of thing.

"What is your name?"

"Laron Gray."

"Where do you stay?"

"About 20 blocks down the street."

"What's the address?"

"I don't know it off the top of my head, I'm not from around here I'm from Ohio." I lied about everything but the house. "I just moved down here a few months ago."

"Do you don't mind if I search your vehicle Mr. Gray?"

"Nope I don't."

He searched my truck and he did not find a thing. I had a key of cocaine in my truck but I had so many secret compartments that I wasn't worried about anything. Now a few more squad cars pulled up with a canine unit to sniff around. I still wasn't worried, I had it in plastic coated with Vaseline and motor oil so the dog will not smell shit.

"It's all clear bub."

He had this look on his face like I had something then a Grand Marquis pulled up and two guys in suits got out and came over to shake my hand.

"How are you doing Mr. Gray?"

"Fine. How about y'all guys?"

"I see you've got yourself into little trouble."

"No not at all they're done and I'm about to go."

"Is that so? Driving without a license is a crime, you could go to jail and your vehicle impounded with hefty fine."

"That's still no trouble playas."

"Oh that is right L-Roy, that ain't about nothing to you."

"L-Roy, who's that?"

"Don't worry, I'll tell y'all fellas."

"You could go we have it from here and throw that ticket it away too while you're at it." "Yeah L-Roy drug dealer, coke pusher, smack banger whatever the nickname is. Your name is ranging. It shocked me the first time I saw you. You're so young and in to what he does. No jewelry nothing flashy, you don't even party all you do is get money. But L-Roy we're on to you and you probably got drugs in your car. Let's just say it's a gift from us to you. Go get right, blowup, we'll be talking to you again. I would give you our cards but a filthy drug dealer won't be putting any type of harassment charges on us today. If you want to know our names you better search. Have a nice day."

"You too guys."

'We will be seeing you again."

"I'll be looking forward to it maybe we could go out to eat and get more acquainted."

"Bye Mr. Gray."

Now as I get back in my whip, I thought about them agents were saying about me being hot out here. I got too much money to be playing around with the streets. Damn here I go with this shit again; I couldn't even hear my phone ringing. "Hello?"

"Yo L, where you at man?"

"I'll be there in about five minutes, I had got pulled over."

"You cool bro?"

"Yeah just some cops all on my dick but I'll holler at you when I get there."

"Alright bro."

That's my main man Devon, a real hustler. I met him selling cell phones on the corner now he's copping bricks off me.

"Let me call this boy and let him know I'm out here."

"Yo you see, aint no need to call me. I saw you I had to take the trash out so my girl wont trip."

"Alright get in."

"What's cracking big homie?"

"You got that money?"

"Yeah 50,000."

"You aint stomp on this shit Devon?"

"Nope."

"That's cool though but the shit could still be broke down two or three more times."

"I'm cool Homie. I feel that raw just like you. I just charge them a little more."

"That's all cool with me but Devon I like you."

"L I fuck with you too."

"Look this is what I'm going to do. This brick is for you, keep your money."

"Why what's up?"

"You going to move up on this list. Whoever I know, you know because you're going to handle all my business dealing with this work."

"But you're not telling me why L-Roy."

"Because I get money and I ain't got time trying to trust the streets so Ima put trust in you. Can handle this work?"

"Okay cool."

Now I put Devon on the whole weight thing. I thought about Jerry, he still didn't hit me back. I'm thinking he might have left and went out of town. He told Tony about what I had done and that did not make no sense to me.

"Look Devon I got a couple sales today. I'm going to introduce you to them so they could get to know you."

"I'm with whatever you're trying to do."

So all day me and Devon was visiting people and serving people and he was pretty cool about it. Onetime I thought he was a little nervous when I told him that we was dropping off 20 bricks. I could see sweat dripping from his head. It was funny to me because I was used to it but it was Devon's first time.

"L-Roy, look I'm not going to disappoint you. I'm a hold it down bro."

"I know that D. What made you break down like that?"

"Because you're the first person whoever gave me anything. The first time you met me whatever I had you were giving me double, then selling me keys of pure cocaine where I could make a killing. Now you're trusting me with major work."

"Man Devon, you're crazy. I been digging you. I thought you had potential and I'm usually right. Look you don't have to hustle with beans and other dudes if you don't want to because I'm a put you on the payroll. How much a week you make right now?"

"About 30 to 40,000 a week."

"Well don't worry about that, I'll pay you 50,000 a week plus bonuses."

"Man L I'm with that."

"Cool and look this is what you do no rocks, no zones, none of that strictly keys. I'm going to step your whole

game up because in 3 to 6 months you should have anywhere from 1 to 2 million in cash. How that sound family?"

"Real nice L."

"Look we going to ride down to the storage place where you could put your work. I own it but I got it in somebody else's name so it will be cool. You won't have to worry about nobody taking nothing. Ima give you this phone with mine and half of Miami's numbers."

As we rode to one of my spots on the Eastside, I stopped passed my crib to give him the phone.

"Hi Tony."

"What's up Devon? Where y'all coming from?"

"Driving around Tony."

"L-Roy?"

"What's up baby?"

"If I died how long would you wait before you got another woman?"

"You know what bae, I never thought about losing you. I seen us getting old and dying together so if you left first I would just be shit out of luck because I don't want no one else but you."

"I hate you L-Roy. You always have the right thing to say."

"That's the truth bae." But in the back of my mind I was

thinking I don't even know this bitch and where that money at. As soon as she slip up she was got both her and uncle Jerry. I thought this while still having a big smile my face.

"Baby could you grab that phone box from under the bed."

"Why can't you do it lazy?"

"Alright don't ask me to get you nothing."

"I don't."

"Fuck you Tony."

"No can't do that baby, I'm on right now."

"Damn every time I come over here you two talk real crazy."

"Devon here I come now. Where is this fucking phone, I know I put it under here. I hate being under this dumbass bed. I'm too big for that. There it go, here cuz."

"Damn L-Roy about time. That's crazy it took you that long."

"Man there's all types of shit under that bed." "Tony clean that shit up."

"What I look like? A maid? She's off for the week."

"And you call me lazy. I'm out bighead. Come give me a kiss before I roll girl."

"Aww ain't that that's so cute."

"Thank you mama. You're crazy alright, one day I ask you for kiss and you runoff now you acting all nice. Bye bae, I love you."

"Love you too L. I like how you did that too."

"Did what?"

"Spun me so I didn't talk."

"Come on Devon while you still got breath."

As we went back outside, I told Devin how to use the phone and what the number to the phone was. We hit the safe spot at my storage room.

"This is it. What do you think?"

"It don't even look like a storage space."

"I know, that's why I keep it like this."

"Do you have a lot of people come here?"

"No just me. All this room but only 4 or 5 have something in them. But we ain't going to worry about that. Let's go find your room. Look room 1010 is yours and guess what the combo is? Take a guess D."

"The same number on my cell phone?"

"That would be hot but nope it's the same as the room number."

"1010?"

"Yep."

"That is hot."

"Now the only thing you have to do is put your thumb on here the computer knows who you are because they're already set for me. Okay now hit 412 then 1010. Here we go now when you come back next time all you do is put your thumb on here and hit 1010 and you will be it right in."

"Damn bro there's a lot of shit in here."

"Yeah yeah look run this room your mind will say this shit is yours and that payroll thing is out the window I was trying to pull you in and I don't want to see you again until the room is empty don't call me about no work man."

"I'm probably be on this for a minute."

"That's what I thought my first time, I was shocked like you. Come on D let's get something to eat."

Now my plan was to send everybody to Devon and let Devon sell all that. I knew he would handle it so all I had to do was send everybody his way. I only have a few months before I go to the burgh and put my brother on something lovely and get my family out the hood.
A week passed by and money was rolling in. Devon was changing; he moved and bought a condo. Now he drives a red Range Rover and two other cars that make him stick

out. He is eating now but one month is not enough time to really start spending money. I don't spend any so I would not know.

"L-Roy, its Devon."

"Tell him to come in bae."

"He is on your phone, it rung so I picked it up. Here."

"Yo what's cracking cuz."

"You already know big Homie. I'm hungry."

"Alright give me a couple minutes and I'll be out."

Now as I brush my teeth, I'm thinking about this flip probably a cool million or more. It's just too easy and it don't seem real but it is what it is. As I get dressed and go outside a jeep rode passed taking some pictures I didn't pay it no mind. I thought it could've been them feds but I'm in too deep. My flip is 20 million every month so I can't act like I'm scared now. That's for the birds, I'm in it to win it.

"What's up L-Roy?"

"What's up you ready pimp?"

"I got two and a half for you player."

"Damn the most I thought I was going to get from you is one and a half."

"I did what you told me to and I stretched that shit." That's how I bought this platinum chain."

"Damn I didn't even see that cuz."

"That's 100 stacks homie. I got the earrings to match and I got a deal on this pinky ring."

"I meant to ask you something, what kind of car is this?"

"You're funny L. A drop top Aston Martin, fully equipped with TVs in all the headrests, PlayStation 2 and Louie everywhere."

"Man you spending big money but if it makes you happy. Take me to the spot. I meant to ask you do you think you ready to play with this dope a little bit?"

"For sure."

"Look Ima give you 10 bricks of dope, you know the rest. That's $1 million from me and like 4 to 8 on the street and it's going to give you 50 bricks of coke."

"I'm ready L."

Now as we go to the storage place I keep seeing the same cars following us. We took so many different cuts to try and lose them that it took us 3 hours to get there. He parked his car and took one of the vans that we put the work in. I drove in behind him in the Austin Martin and it was alright. I'm used to driving my truck all the time that it made it feel funny to drive something so new and fast.

After I dropped Devon and his car off, me and Tony decided to rent some movies and cuddle up in front of the TV. I forgot to put the money up and brought it in with me; I was in my lazy mood. I figured I had nothing to do

tomorrow so that would be the first thing on my list to do. Then a knock at the door came out of nowhere and took me out my kung fu mode.

"Who is it?"

"Who you think young buck?"

"I know that ain't Jerry."

"Is the door locked?"

"Yeah or I would've been came in."

As I walked to the door I tripped over my shoes and hit my big toe and it made me mad as fuck.

"What's up uncle Jerry?"

"Come on I got something for you."

"What is it?"

"Well if I was planning on telling you I would have so. Go get dressed and we are going out."

"But uncle Jerry."

"You have been getting money all day and all week and every day of the month. Let's take some time off. Now go get ready."

"Alright give me a couple minutes because Tony was looking forward to this night and I know she's going to be pissed off."

"Go ahead and do your thing. I will be out front."

Now in my head I know Tony ain't trying to hear none of this because I've been gone all day every day. I know she's going to snap out. On my way back to the room I thought about what I was going to say even if it didn't sound too good.

"Hey bae."

"What is it now L-Roy? I see my uncle came in to say hi so I know the two of you are up to something but I don't know what it is so go ahead and spit it out."

"Well bae it's like this your uncle wants to show me something. He wants me to get dressed so he can take me to wherever or whatever he's going to show me."

"Look L I'm not going to get in your way right now but do take some time out for me okay."

"No doubt."

"You know why right?"

"Of course."

"No you don't. Be quiet and come here and I will show you."

"What, no don't do that." but before I could say anything else Tony was unzipping my pants and sucking my dick relentlessly. We haven't had sex in a while so I came fast; she was so good at making me cum fast. As soon as she finished I got dressed and was out the door. Jerry had a

load of women in the excursion.

"You ready, we going to hit the club first then a couple other places. I want you to meet my friends. Let me introduce you to the ladies. L-Roy this is Mimi, Black Cherry, Tiffany and Kelly."

"Hi, how ya'll doing?" I couldn't help but stare they were all fine as fuck looking like models.
I haven't danced in a while but it was time for me to have some fun. We pulled up in front of the club it was only a couple blocks away as with everything else in Miami. It was packed, cars and people everywhere. I was like damn this is about to go down. As we are looking for a parking spot, I hear this voice from the back of the music.

"L-Roy would you dance with me?"

"Black Cherry yes I'm sorry of course I will."

"I know all of them women are going to be all over you and I at least want to get the first dance."

"Black I don't think they're going to be all over me like that."

"Yeah okay, you'll see."

I'm saying to myself all them balling ass dudes in here, you're not going to be paying me any attention.

"Here you go."

"What's this Jerry?"

"The vip passes baby, we do it real big when we go out."

So we went in through the back door and went up to this room with a spinning ball. There were strippers and all kinds of bottles of stuff I never drank before. There was Cristal, pills on the table, bowls of that shit and dudes with stacks of money in front of them giving it to women to strip for them and give them lap dances. A few chicks asked to give me a dance but I was cool besides I brought 5k with me that's just so I won't be broke and I'm not really going to spend it.

"Come on L-Roy."

"Talk to me girl."

"Let's go downstairs and get our dance on."

"I'm with it. Jerry we going to go downstairs."

"Holla youngin."

"Come on L-Roy this is my song."

So I went to the dance floor and she was freaking the shit out of me. Black Cherry was bad, she was black alright and I bet her pussy was probably as red as a cherry. This girl's body was on point and my dick was hard the whole time dancing with her. I felt so embarrassed but she was rubbing that ass on it and she wouldn't stop. She had the nerve to ask me if I like the way she danced, she knew I did. I told her what she wanted to hear anyways and she just smiled at me. Now I knew I could've fucked her but I was cool and MOB is what I'm on money over bitches and

niggas. After we got done dancing she started asking questions.

"Do you have a woman L-Roy?"

"Yeah we live together."

"You love her?"

"Yeah that's my baby."

"Are you always this quiet?"

"Most of the time. There's usually nothing to talk about but I'm trying to talk to you sexy as long as it's not about sex or about me and you being together."

"That's fine with me but why you say it like that?"

"Well it's like this me and my woman are doing pretty good together and I'm not trying to fuck that up. Even if she doesn't know, I will know. Oh and another thing is we could be friends if you promise to be good."

"You're so sweet L-Roy. I will be happy just to be your friend and I will be good."

"Promise?"

"I promise."

"Okay that's what I'm talking about."

Now as we continue to get freaky on the dance floor, Black Cherry was licking all on me and whispering in my ear, I thought it was cute so I just let her do her. We went

back to the vip lounge and got a few drinks, well she did not me. I just watched, even Jerry got pissy drunk and was touching all on the women, I guess he was a regular there because they just smiled when he touched every area of their body. After doing all that dancing, I was hungrier than a fat person.

"Black you hungry?"

"Hell yeah, they got some bomb ass wings."

"You're as funny as hell. I want some ribs or something. Let's get everybody and go hit a rib shop."

As we try to round everybody up, Mimi is the only one we got to wait on because she's getting her pussy ate by some dude in the club.

"Damn could you tell him to hurry up."

"He's paying, he could take as long as he wants."

"Well we're out."

As we were walking back to the whip, me and Jerry are arguing over who's driving. This went on for 20 minutes before he gave up and I was so fucking hungry. I was driving down the road with the music blasting, I really wasn't paying attention. Most of the time I'm on point but not today. Right before we got to the red light a blue van pulled up in front of us blocking our path and another one pulled up in back of us. I could not back out of there, we were stuck.

Before they had a chance to get out the whip, I

already pulled out my baby nine from under the passenger seat and told everyone to run. I never looked back; I was out the whip and blasting at the van in the front. I saw they were fully strapped with AKs but it didn't matter, I was almost around a building when the shots rang out. I was grazed on the side of my head but it wasn't about nothing. I could tell one of them dudes was on me so I hit a few more cuts and ducked behind some cars and sent a few shots at the two guys who were following me. I could tell one got hit but the other one was chewing every thang up in my area so I had to get out of there. Now after running for a couple more blocks I saw the police coming in my direction so I threw the gun under a parked car and kept walking. Just as I thought they pulled right up on me.

"Did you hear any gun shots sir?"

"I sure did, they sound like they were coming from down there."

"Well sir you better get inside, we are going to be blocking these streets off."

"Yes sir." And I kept moving.

After I went back and got my gun, I got a little lost it took me 45 minutes to make it to my house and when I did get there Tony was wide awake still watching movies. Everything was all right until I turned on the light.

"Oh baby don't move."

"Why?"

"Just lay down."

"Tony, why are you crying?"

"Your heads bleeding. It looks like…wait you were shot?"

"Baby I'm ok, it just grazed me."

"You were out with my uncle, you come back by yourself and almost got killed or something. What happened?"

"We were car jacked and it got out of control."

"Well where is my uncle at?"

"I don't know."

"What do you mean you don't know?"

"I don't know. I started shooting and got up out of there. That's why I turned the light on so I could try and find my keys."

"Come on we could take my car, he might be hurt or something."

"We jumped in the whip and started to drive the route I ran from. We didn't see no one but police and Jerry wasn't answering his phone. I could tell Tony was nervous about not finding her uncle but there was nothing I could do about that."

"Why did you leave him L-Roy?"

"Because the guys that pulled up on us were heavily armed and all I had on me was my nine so I told everyone to get

out and run. I started shooting and got out of there myself. They could've got away maybe but I never looked back until I got up the street because they were still following me."

"Damn L-Roy, I wish you could've still been with my uncle."

"Me too but the situation did not let us be together."

So we are riding around every part of town to see if we could find Jerry when my phone rings.

"Hello?"

"Where you at L?"

"Nowhere, where you at J?"

"I'm at…"

"Is that Jerry?"

"Yeah he's trying to tell me…"

"Let me see that phone!"

"Here man because you are not going to be getting on my nerves."

"Uncle Jerry, where are you at?"

"Right down the street from the rib shack on 7th and long."

"Why didn't you answer the phone when we called you?"

"Oh I didn't hear it ring."

"Are you ok?"

"Yeah when we got out most of the guys went after L-Roy so we ran around the corner and jumped back in the car a drove off. Now come up to the rib shop."

"Uh no Me and L-Roy are going home, we will see you tomorrow. Bye."

"We are going home L-Roy."

"I'm alright with that. He alright?"

"Yes, he said most of the guys ran after you so they had time to get back in the car and drive away. You did help them baby."

"Don't baby me now just take me home so I could get some sleep."

"Aww you're a big baby, naw, I'm just playing with you sexy."

Damn I could've died so I decided it was time for me to get up out of the MIA asap so I could see my family. I decided in the morning I would tell Devon I was rolling but I would still keep in touch and let my uncle Jerry know I was gone. So when me and Tony went back to the house she did what she always does but I wasn't in the mood for that after what just happened.

CHAPTER 11

"Good morning honey."

"What happened?"

"You were knocked out as soon as you l got on the bed."

"I don't even remember that, only me telling you to get off me. By the way bae, I'm going up to the burgh for a few months."

"The burgh like Pittsburgh?"

" Yeah."

"For what?"

"To see my family."

"Why don't you just wait a few more months and we could go up together."

"Naw I'm cool, I want to go now. Where my phone?"

"On the couch and don't go home and do nothing crazy L-Roy."

"I'm not."

So as I walk away from Tony and go to call Devon, I hear footsteps. "Who's that?"

"It's me Jerry. Who else would just walk in your house."

"Bad timing, I'm out, I'm going to holla at my peoples back home."

"That's fine you need a vacation."

"Ima drive up and take some work with me. Ima take Devon with me too, I'll be in touch."

"Alright call me if you need something L-Roy."

"I got you J."

"Hi Tony."

"Hi uncle Jerry."

"Bye Tony."

"Bye uncle Jerry."

"Alright L call me when you touch down."

"Cool."

So as I call Devon, he lets it ring for a while before he

picks up.

"What's up L-Roy, It's a little early."

"I'm about to roll up to Pittsburgh and I want you to ride with me."

"No doubt."

"Well get dressed and I'll holla about the rest when I get there."

I pack up my clothes and hit the road. I just left out the door because I knew Tony would've talked my head off; I knew that for a fact.

As I drove to Devon's house I thought about what I was going to say to my brother and my mom and how to break it down to them I was a millionaire. I know it would be a shock to them, but it's true. Let me call this nigga, damn here he go again.

"Yo you ready?"

"Naw give me like 5 more minutes, I was in the shower."

"Alright just make sure you pack up and lock up cuz we out."

"Alright bro."

After I get off the phone with Devon, I call to rent some cars.

"Hello this is high drive cars how may I help you?"

"I need 2 midsize cars with full coverage and I need them for 3 months."

"Ok sir I see you already have an account with us so will just charge it to your card, what time will you be picking them up?"

"In about 15 to 25 minutes."

"Ok Mr. Gray they will be ready for you."

"Thank you."

"You're welcome sir."

I went and grabbed about 10 keys from the warehouse and about 10 stacks. I was used to living a certain way and I know the projects would get on my last nerve so I was going to stay in a hotel. I never put 10 bricks in my stash spot only 3 or 4 at a time and come to find out only 8 of them fit. Bad enough I'm riding dirty now it's even worse with 2 keys under my seat. Fuck it that's why I have to put more people on but I don't want to get cased up. Let me stop trippin and go get Devon. Now I know I got 10 bricks in my whip but that wasn't why I was trippin it's because those 2 little bricks was talking to every under cover and cop that rode by me. I rode with over 100 bricks before so this aint nothing new but the whole way to Devon's house I was scared to death. I made it and Devon was still getting ready. I wanted to cuss him out when he picked up the phone but I just let it go.

"What up D, I'm out front."

"Yeah my bad I'm still getting my clothes together."

"Come on dog I'm out here slippin."

"Here I come bro."

See that's the shit I'm talking about, dudes always taken all day and that's how they are with everything in life and they end up being in the way and right now Devon's in my way. I don't like his style anyway, he's too flashy and I know he's going to bring a lot of heat in the long run so when I get to where I gotta get I'm a drop him off.

"Yo bro, help me with these bags."

See this is the shit I'm talking about.

"Got Damn where are you going?"

"Man I aint trying to spend a lot of money when we down ya way."

"Man you been spending money, why you want to change now."

"Bro just put these in the truck for me please."

"Yeah I got you."

"That's what's up. Look D I just wanted you to hurry up because I'm riding with 2 keys under my seat and 8 more in my stash spot."

"Oh why didn't you say that?"

"Because we were on the phone and you don't know who

could be listening to our conversation."

"My bad bro. Look lets be out."

"That's what I'm talking about and roll that window up I got the AC on."

Now as we ride to get the rentals that I have to fix up so the bricks stay hidden, I'm talking to Devon about the plan and he's just half into it but I aint worried about it he's not going to be around long no way.

'Yo L where we at?"

"You aint been listening to anything I've been saying, this is the rental place, I told them I was on the way."

"What kind of cars you get bro?"

"Why?"

"Damn dog I was just asking L-Roy."

"Probably 2 Maxima's or 2 Camry's."

"Oh that's cool."

Now I'm saying to myself this nigga stupid, he acts like a fucking child that just got some money.

"Mr. Gray?"

"Yes."

"Hello sir your cars are right there. Now I know who you are but I still need your credit card sir."

"That's fine, here you go."

"Look Devon follow me to this parking lot so I could park this ride."

"No doubt baby."

I know I shouldn't be driving this fast but I'm just trying to hurry up but we made it to the parking lot without seeing one cop on the street. Now I changed the floor in the rental and put a drop floor in there that moves from a button number with 3 digits that's hid inside the horn of the car.

Once everything was done we went back to get the other ride and we tossed coins to see who would drive the car with the coke in it and Devon won the luxury of driving with the drugs. Well I cheated a little but he would never know that coin was tails on both sides and I would never tell him. Now we hit the highway flying on 95 North up through ATL then South Carolina. The gas tanks were full and we had extra gas in the trunks so we wouldn't have to do much stopping. We had to stop in South Boston Virginia it was no problem. We stopped ate at white castle and got gas and was out. We were traveling on 79 North on our way to Pittsburgh with no sleep. We've been on the road for 14 hours and now had 3 to 4 more to go. When we finally got to Pittsburgh, I called Devon on the phone and told him to use all of his turn signals, don't stop and pay close attention the road because they lock people up quickly here.

"Look bro be cool."

"I'm sleepy but I'm not that sleepy."

No more than 20 minutes went past and this nut went to sleep right at the light. Now I have to jump out the whip and wake this fool up.

"Yo D wake up nigga, wake up."

"Man I'm woke."

"Nigga you was sleep."

"Damn for real?"

"Just pay attention cuz."

"Alright Alright."

"Cool D?"

"Yeah yeah."

No sooner than I closed the door the police pulled right up on us. My heart dropped.

"Is everything alright here?"

"Yes officer my friend is just a little tired and I just got out to let him know we'll be there in about 10 minutes."

"I see your license plates say Florida, where are you headed?"

"I'm from the city right on the North Side. And yes they do, I was just down there on vacation and rented these cars from drive back home."

"Ok drive safely and have a nice day."

"Thanks officer you too."

I hurried up and got in my car and went from downtown, I crossed the bridge and headed to the north side to my mom's house. When I pulled up I saw house was burned down. I didn't even stop to say hi to anyone, I've been away a year and my mom moved. The only thing I could think of was the house caught fire and she moved to another part of the hood, like anyone else from Northview Heights. So I drove down to my block you know 7 court or 700 block. Now when me and Devon drove around there shit looked different, young girls got a little older, young dudes were driving and the block was packed so when we pulled up dudes didn't even move. We got out and niggas went crazy.

"Yo L-Roy where you been at cuz? Niggas is looking for you, we all were."

"What's up?"

"Ya mom and ya brother is gone man, dead."

"How what happened?"

"Your mom was in a fire, they say them dudes from the hill you were feuding with set it and your brother was burned up too. They caught him slipping at club laga. Ya cuz from Hoodtown was with him you know who we talking about."

"Yeah where he at?"

"They caught him slippin out Homestead at Lowes theatre shot him in his face 17 times. He had a closed casket. Cuz there are some up sides. Most of them niggas are dead, the one who killed ya cuz got life plus 20 to 40. You won't see none of them niggas no more."

"Damn Mark."

"Don't cry cuz it aint your fault."

"But it is Ray J, I wasn't here to hold them down, now they're gone."

"Damn L sorry to hear that L. So you know what you have to do family?"

"What Devon?"

"Get rich, not just for your loved ones but for the hood to pick them up out this rut."

"No doubt I'm going harder than I ever did."

CHAPTER 12

I put Devon down with the hood let him meet everybody that mattered. I bought a crib out Ambridge to lay down at and found a nice storage spot out Monroeville to put my coke at. Now at first it was tough because I got major work and dudes was nervous to fuck with it. But after one month, I was going back and forth to Miami bringing up a hundred bricks at a time, the hood loved me and the people that wasn't down with me, I got them knocked off. Get down or lay down like them JBM dudes from Philly, the hood was poppin we had everything, crack, coke, dope, weed, wet, whatever you wanted I had it even pussy. Once my money got up passed 10 million without having to mess with it to flip, I started small putting store busses in the hood, ice-cream trucks and going to construction spots with lunch trucks. It was going good. I gave a lot of people in the hood jobs but I needed more, I felt like I owed my mom TJ and cuz Mark more than that. So I

started safe streets for kids where they clean up the neighborhood get help with their school work, clothing allotments to get their gear and take trips anywhere in the US once a month. It was cool then I started my own rap label, NVH records, and for the first time in my life I was happy. After finding out everyone I loved in my world was gone, I broke down and asked Sharon to marry me. We were starting to get cool when I came back and we started going out. What it was she felt bad about what happened but it was the love I needed and we did it right at Disney World. It was great I invited over 3 thousand people. Tony was just a ghost to me, I even got my number changed. I still wasn't flashy. I even bought my hood and police wasn't just allowed to ride through my neighborhood, I could say that now my hood worked for me, Laron Gray, a little boy who had star written all on his face. Everything was going good but I just couldn't take it. Knowing that Shady was still alive while my family was dead. So I put a million dollars on Shadys head and in about a week Shady was no more but it still didn't take the pain away. It just made me step my game up, I was shooting a video in the hood, my first one, and the label was doing well with the mix tapes and had a few singles. It made close to 3 million but now it was time to get on TV and get my clothing line out there. Everything went good and in about a month we were on 106 and my video was on the countdown, it was like a dream come true.

"Introducing the CEO of NVH records, L-Rizzy the don."

The crowd went crazy, we came out like 20 deep wearing Steelers jerseys and Pirates shirts.

"What's up tigga?"

"What up L-Rizzy."

"You know holding it down."

"So tell the crowed something about yourself."

"Well I'm 27 I'm from Pittsburgh, PA shouts out to all my niggas from the North Side and all over. I got more music, more artists coming out, and more money to make. Oh yeah I brought shoes and shirts from my new clothing line, All Out Wear, and I brought everyone a candy bar because I do have a candy bar called Millennium Bar out."

"So I see you're into a little bit of everything."

"And look out for my new book too and for anyone who wants to ask L-Rizzy the Don a simple question, you could reach me at www.lrizzythedongetmoney.net any time and if you come to Pittsburgh in the next few years I will be opening up a mini mall, a hot new club and a hotel so just be ready to have a ball when you come to my hood."

"So L-Rizzy you pretty much told us everything."

"Naw that wasn't nothing, just a small part."

"So L go ahead and welcome your video on 106 and park for the first time."

"Well the new joint of the day is my joint featuring B-Real, Sheena and Bay Bay in it, it's called holla at me. So holla at me 106 and park."

It was great when I got back to the hood everybody was talking about that. All I could do was tell them praise God and everybody was like yeah praise him bro he is worthy no doubt.

Then I got a call from Rudy telling me that Devon got popped on the South Side with three keys of coke. The fiend he was serving turned out to be an undercover federal agent so I called Jerry and asked him what he thought I should do but he didn't answer two days straight. I thought he was mad at me something. When I tried the last time he picked up.

"Jerry!"

"What's up L I aint head from you in a while, I hope you're getting that money."

"You know that J."

"So what's up with you and Tony?"

"It wasn't working."

"That's cool I still fuck with you L you don't have to say no more."

"Look my man was popped with a couple of keys from an undercover federal agent."

"L get him out then kill him, he's probably talking to them already."

"I will call you later J."

"Handle that don't be playing around."

"I got you."

"No you better have yourself before you be doing a long time."

"I got you, one."

Fuck now I gotta get this nigga out, let me think, what should I do first, ok ok, I'm a call Shay tell him go pay Devon's bond no matter what, then holla at Ray J and have him put in that work for me. Damn where's my other fucking phone, oh yeah its out in my car, I just bought a new Chrysler 300c. I just went to sleep in there and left everything in that bitch when I went in to find Jerry's number. Damn here it goes. Now as I Call Shay my minds thinking if he brought my name up and if they're already on me.

"Yo what's up bro, this L-Roy."

"What's crackin cuz?"

"How much is Devon's bond cuz?"

"He aint got one."

"Yeah I heard the Feds be doing that shit."

"No doubt L."

"Well if he call back tell him we can't do nothing right now."

"Alright cuz."

"Alright Shay."

"What's up cuz?"

"Damn Ray J you scared the shit out of me, don't be doing that man."

"My bad homie."

"Naw its cool, I was about to call you anyway."

"For what L?"

"That nigga Devon."

"Yeah what about him?"

"He got nabbed with some bricks that he slung to a federal agent."

"You know he might drop a dime right."

"You think?"

"So L?"

"Yeah?"

"That nigga aint never do no time before."

"Look when that nigga get out were going to throw him a good bye party, you feel me cuz."

"Flat out L, just give me the word."

Days passed like any others, getting money and fucking bitches, a few new motherfuckers moved in my

hood. I told my niggas to keep an eye on them and don't nobody sell them any weight and I put females on the ones old enough to get in the game. One night out on the block, Just Chillen, Devon pulls up in a brand new Bentley and jumps out with all of this jewelry on like he's a fucking rap star or something.

"Yeah what it is niggas."

"That nigga home, about time." Sheena says.

"You've been ok, you just stopped calling."

"Yeah I was stressed out ya'll. L what's up homie?"

"Chillen just mad I couldn't get you out homie."

"Man don't worry about it. My lawyer says it won't stick, it was entrapment so he tells me the most I could get is 5 years, at the most a mandatory 3 for some shit he was saying. But that aint about nothing."

In the back of my head I'm saying that nigga dropped a dime and he won't be alive after today. So we went out, first to Dave and Busters then to the club. Got with some hoes, hit the second time around out homestead, it was stripper night and Devon was spending big money on these hoes. They were loving him, I was even happy because I always thought this nigga drew too much attention. Now while Devon is playing with this stripper bitches pussy, I called Ray J. Pick up please, pick up.

"Hello?"

"What up bro was you sleep?"

"Yeah but I'm woke now."

"Remember what we talked about?"

"No doubt."

"It's on for sure."

"Where L?"

"Look that fiend Tammy at the bottom of Hazlet get her crib, that's where the party is going to be at. Let everybody know real quick, grab a DJ and tell dudes its free with all you can drink and smoke. You got 3 hours to get this shit together."

"Alright."

"I'll holla at you about the rest face to face. Oh yeah Ray J?"

"What?"
"Let everybody know we are throwing it for Devon and have everyone scream welcome home when he comes through."

"No doubt."

"I'll get at you."

"For sure L."

In the meantime me and Devon get drunk and spend money. I know I can't handle my Henny but I keep downing it like its water and slip up and start talking to some fools I don't even know about that money when in

fact they were on me the whole time because Devon gave them my name, Federal agents. I was joking and talking to these fools like we were the best of friends and I didn't even ask their names but the words were flowing.

"So L-Roy how much them things go for, them bricks them whole ones, them chickens give me some prices."

Now even though I was drunk, I still didn't give up anything to let them know I have the work."

"I heard in the street people were saying they wanted 50 thousand for one."

"Well who L-Roy?"

"Man I don't know, I don't hustle and I don't know anybody who's moving that much work."

"What! L-Roy they say the Northside running things."

"For one why ya mans so quiet and what's ya'll name."

"Well my name is Brah."

"And what's your friend's name?"

"My name is Mike."

"Well it was nice talking to ya'll."

"Hopefully we'll meet again L-Roy."

"Maybe."

"L-Roy?"

"What's up Mike?"

"I will see you again for sure."

Now taking down drinks and talking to them fools time flew by.

"Devon lets go."

"Naw bro I'm taking this chick with us."

"I don't care, you're a grown ass man."

"No doubt pimpin."

Now as Devon picks this broad up and puts her in the Benz, I told them to sit in the backseat and do their thing. No faster than Project Pat came on Devon was down in the back seat eating this bitches pussy. I'm looking at her eyes in the rearview and she just keeps winking at me. I just keep laughing. We were on the Northside in a matter of 15 to 20 minutes and this nigga just start fucking this broad no rub or nothing. I grab my phone and call Ray J who's on my speed dial.

"Yo what's up bro?"

"We are at the bottom of Penfort get everybody ready."

"We're ready."

"Look I'm turning on Mount Pleasant right now. Can you see me right now, I'm turning on Hazlet."

"I see you cuz."

"Alright Ray, one. Pimp come on Devon, you ready."

"Where we going?"

"There's a party and everyone's supposed to be there."

"I'm with that, what about you baby?"

"I'm with you daddy."

Now as we get out the car and walk over to the party as soon as we walked through the door.

"Surprise! Welcome home Devon."

"L-Roy you put this together?"

"No doubt baby. Yo Devon Ima get at you, Ima go get on some of these honeys in here."

"For sure playa, for sure."

I walk away from Devon looking for Ray J and not no dumb ass broads finally finding him in the basement of the house.

"Ray J what's up?"

"I'm ready bro."

"Look one shot to the head bro. You bang that D E I bought you."

"No doubt L."

"Well look, make sure aint nobody outside. Go get dressed

in some black shit and make sure your face is covered. One shot cuz."

"I got you L."

"Call me when you're ready and I will bring him out back."

"Alright I'm out."

Now I'm going to find Devon and when I do he's drunk to the core. So I had to convince him to come outside.

"Hold on let me answer my phone Devon."

"Yo it's me."

"You see us."

"For sure."

"I'm going in talk to you later Ray."

"For sure."

"Devon. I'm going to light this blunt real quick I'll be right back out."

"No doubt homie."

"Yo L-Roy where Devon at?"

"Aint he upstairs bae." I replied to the stripper chick he brought with him.

"No I checked."

"Did you check the bathroom?"

"No, but…"

"He might be in there you know he's drunk."

"You're right, you're right."

"Well get on with it."

"Damn where the fuck is this nigga L-Roy at I'm trying to get my smoke on and I left that little bitch and my drink upstairs."

"Yo, what's up homie?"

"Who that?'

That's the last words Devon ever said as he was shot in his head, pockets turned out and raped for his jewels, dead with a big hole in his head. He was out there for a while because I turned the music up and got the crowd rowdy and interested in what I was doing, clowning that's all.

Right before I was about to holla at this chick in these tight ass pants, my phone rang.

"Yo it's done L."

"I'll holla at you tomorrow J."

Now it's time for me to get ready to roll but somebody has to find that body, someone who don't know nothing. Oh this dumb ass stripper broad.

"Yo what's up boo, you trying to smoke?"

"For sure."

"Look lets go out back because there's a lot of dudes in here who want to hit some of this purple. So go out back and light it up and I will go grab us some more of that punch."

"Ok boo."

As soon as I got to the top of the steps all I heard was screams. Ray J must've killed him right in front of the door because chicky never closed it. Now everyone was going outside but not me. I was out the door, right in Devon's 600 and right to my crib and into my bed.

CHAPTER 13

"Somebody call 911."

"I already called them."

"He was just like this?"

"Yes."

"Who are you?"

"Just a friend of Devon's I was about to come out here and smoke a blunt when I seen Devon's head wide open and blood everywhere that's when I screamed."

"Did you see anybody?"

"Excuse me who are you. You're not the police."

"Oh no baby I'm not, I'm the owner of this house. Just call me Auntie, look here come the police. Just answer their questions and then I will see if I could get someone

to take you home.'

'Ok auntie."

Now as the police arrived no one seen anything or heard anything. After that night I put the clamps on the hood, I knew the feds would be coming around here trying to get as much drugs as possible because their main informant is now dead and I don't serve no one anything.

One day Sheena, Sharon's sister, wanted to smoke a blunt of this new batch of chocolate dro I brought to the hood. I rarely smoke in the ride but it was still Devon's 600 Benz so I did it. I only had a half ounce on me so I wasn't worried about police. We are driving around the Northside and Sheena wanted to give me some head while I was driving. She said she never did that before and she told me she never been with a millionaire.

"Sheena you fucked me before though."

"Yeah but that was before you were rich L-Roy."

"Alright."

I let her suck my dick, she was good at it but it wasn't like before when I was younger. I had a baby by her sister and we were married. I rode, smoked and got hit and she didn't want to stop so I let her continue. Now before I could bust this second nut an unmarked car was pulling me over and forcing me and Sheena to get out the car.

"Would you step outside the car sir?"

"For what and who are ya'll?"

"FBI sir."

"Could I see some badges, ya'll might be trying to rob me or something."

"Well how's this, I'm Agent Miller and you already know Detectives Faulk and Jones."

"No can't say that I do."

"Well they know you. Now Mr. Gray do you know the owner of this car?"

"For sure."

"Do you know where he is at now?"

"Well I was told through the grapevine he was killed."

"Do you know anything about it?"

"Nope."

"Where were you at when he got killed?"

"Well at first I was at the party, then I went home."

"Who were you with?"

"Well the girl that I was with, they said after I left found the body."

"Look Mr. Gray we want to take you down to the Federal Building."

"For what?"

"We just want to ask you some more questions, but your friend could go."

"Look Sheena tell everybody where I'm at and don't give nobody the whip."

"Ok bae, I got you."

Now they put me in the back of the car and take me down to the Federal Building to try and make a fool out of me but everybody knows I'm a G.

"Yo Ray J, is that Sheena driving the Benz?"

"Fuckin right Shay."

"Man flag that bitch down."

"Yo Sheena."

"What's up Shay?"

"Ray J wants you."

"OK, tell him here I come."

"Naw he wants to talk to you now."

"Ok. Yeah what's up Ray J.?"

"What's up my ass, what the fuck you doing driving L-Roy shit bitch?"

"Look let me explain."

"Well talk hoe."

"Me and L-Roy was pulled over by homicide and the feds."

"For what?"

"About that shit that happened with Devon."

"Shit did they cuff him?"

"No they just said they wanted to ask him some questions but they said I could go and L-Roy told me to come back to the hood and don't let nobody have the whip."

"No doubt, I respect that I just hope they don't try no slick shit."

"But L-Roy said he seen it coming Shay."

"Yeah he be alright.

CHAPTER 14

"So Mr. Gray, what type of relationship did you and Mr. Fuller have?"

"Who Devon? Oh me and him was good friends."

"Have you ever sold him any drugs?"

"Nope not that I could remember, neither me nor Devon sold drugs."

"Well how do you think he got that nice car of his?"

"I don't know, you tell me."

"From the drugs you were giving him."

"Nope, have you ever seen me in a nice car? No you haven't even when I'm allowed to ride like that if I want to when I'm worth 15 million in the bank legally."

"That's true Mr. Gray we haven't seen you do anything, we haven't heard anything about you through the grapevine as

you say but we were wondering where all these drugs are coming from until we caught your main man Devon red handed and he told us everything about your little operation but he didn't know who your connection was other than that or we would've came and picked you up then. Now you can make it easy on yourself and tell us who you are getting these drugs from and maybe you could get back on the streets in about 10 years or we could let you go and keep watching you and wait for you to slip up."

"Agent Miller I don't sell drugs so that second proposal sounds pretty good to me."

"Well Mr. Gray you could go or should we call you L-Roy."

"Hey man it is what it is but I'm a grown ass man and I would like if you called me Mr. Gray."

"Have a nice day Mr. Gray."

"And please don't harass me that will look nasty in court if I have to put restraining orders on you guys."

"Don't worry Mr. Gray we're not coming unless we have something."

"Good day guys."

"Good day Mr. Gray. Oh Mr. Gray its funny how Mr. Devon was killed no more than a day after getting out."

"I just hope ya'll find the killer before I do."

Now as I leave the Federal Building from down Manchester on the Northside, I called up Sheena's house to tell her to come and pick me up. I could have called anybody but the Feds could still be watching me and I didn't want them to see my team.

"Hello, hi how are you doing Ms. Victoria."

"Yes baby."

"Tell Sheena to meet me in front of the 7-11 down Manchester."

"OK, oh L-Roy?"

"Yes ma'am."

"Sharon came passed with the baby."

"Did she say where she was going?"

"No but I think Shawn was going to take her out to eat because she was talking about being hungry."

"Thanks."

"Bye baby and be safe."

"Yes ma'am."

As I walk down to 7-11 I just thought about some hoagie shit and I decided to run down to subway. On my way down to subway, I was just thinking about all the money I made over the years and all the people I helped and if I should just stop and go legal but my heart won't let me. I'm stuck in the middle at this time. Now me being in

la la land I didn't see this red Lex truck do a u turn and speeding in my direction. Now when I snapped out of dreamland I just saw a window coming down and a gun being pointed out the window at me. As sparks come out the barrel of the AK I just remembered everything looking like a movie and moving so slow, it seemed like I couldn't run faster. They were just stuck where they were at, sending shots at me round after round. When it finally stopped and what happened after that I don't remember because I passed out from all the blood I lost and was in the hospital. When I finally woke up I couldn't move and my stomach all the way up to my neck was wrapped up so I thought I was paralyzed. After talking to the nurse, I found out I was hit in my back and the drugs were doing that to me, making me unable to move.

"Excuse me nurse, how long have I been here?"

"About 3 days Mr. um…Gray."

"Has anyone been here to see me?"

"Yes a woman and her son, her name is on the list out front Mr. Gray, would you like to know?"

"No ma'am it was my woman."

"That's what I thought also, she was very pretty."

"Thanks Mrs."

"You could call me Asia and not Mrs. Anything, I'm only 27 Mr. Gray."

"And I'm only 23 and you could call me L-Roy sexy."

"Well thanks Mr. I mean L-Roy."

"Look Asia give me a pen and a piece of paper."

"Oh why?"

"So I could call you for sure."

"Give me it and I will put it in my phone."

"Alright what is it L-Roy?"

"412-377-3242."

"Alright bae I got you."

"Man get at me cuz you sexy as fuck."

"L-Roy I been knowing who you were, I just never met you or talked to you before."

"Oh you're from the Northside?"

"Ya I'm from Hoodtown."

"For real?"

"No for fake, yeah dummy I'm from Hoodtown."

"Who you be with down there?"

"I aint into that life and I don't really have any friends but that's where I live and I still live on Samsonia st. I did stay on Jacksonia."

"Damn I aint never seen you before. What you work out or something?"

"Yeah something like that boo but I will come back tonight and I will show you how I work out. When I was washing you up I seen that big ass dick you got."

"I hope you wasn't playing with it."

"I was tempted but I said I will wait until he wake up to see how much of that snake could fit in my mouth and I swallow everything boo. I know you're going to choke me a little bit but it will be worth it and when you get better I will let you tear my back out."

"For sure I'm with that, look shut the door Asia."

"For what?"

"I want you to come beat my dick for me then pull your pants down and let me put it in your ass."

"Bae you're crazy."

"Are you with it?"

"Yeah bae."

"Well come on."

"OK."

"Sharon is L-Roy ok."

"Yeah mom."

"Did you go get that boys car off Sheena before that girl tear it up?"

"Yes mom. But mom?"

"What baby?"

"Do you think me and L-Roy will last?'

"Well boo I don't know. When ya'll were younger ya'll did not get along, he had sex with your sister before, everybody wants to be with him and he's rich and still married you. So I could say ya'll have a strong chance."

"Yeah he just don't pay me enough attention."

"Well baby the boy is busy think about it he owns the neighborhood, he's the ceo of his own rap label, he helps the kids with his nonprofit organization, he owns real estate, store buses, lunch trucks, ice-cream trucks, his own clothing line, his own shoes, a candy bar and the other street stuff that we know about and he's always on TV and he's married with a child and now he's in the hospital. Now you tell me how much time did you think you were going to get from him?"

"But mom."

"But nothing close your mouth and open your legs and mouth girl and play your part and if that boy ask you for some asshole you better drop it like it's hot."

"Come on mom you're a little deep aren't you."

"No that's your husband he wants to go deep not me."

"But Uncle Jerry I'm ok down here without him."

"I thought you love him."

"Yeah but he don't love me."

"So you're just going to sit around the house and get fat."

"Well everybody said I need to gain weight."

"But not like this Tony, I'll be over in about 15 minutes."

"For what?"

"Damn I'm not allowed over?"

"Of course you are but what are you trying to do?"

"Take you out, spend some money on my niece because you're too much of a beauty to be by yourself."

"Go like where, maybe I don't know for real Uncle Jerry."

"Is my name Jerry?"

"Well it's on youngin."

"Bye Uncle Jerry."

"That niece of mine so much to offer but has no fight in her." Jerry mumbles to himself. "Bye baby see you in 15."

Now as me and Asia finish up our cum bash, I was ready to be out the hospital. I knew they weren't going to let me go so I called Ray J to come get me. When Ray J popped up he told me how them dumb ass cops were running through the city trying to find answers. I never told no one about the problem me and TJ had on the hill

but what Ray J was about to say would speed my heart right up.

"L-Roy."

"What's up cuz? You sayin my name like you just found out what it was."

"Naw I meant to tell you something I forgot because it's been so long."

"Spit it out."

"Remember that mac you had."

"For sure."

"You know it got sucked up a while back."

"Man that aint about nothing."

"Naw cuz that's not the major part."

"Damn what else could it be?"

"When that mac went to ballistics it was a match to them cops who got killed a while back on the hill."

"So, a lot of guns have bodies on them."

"Naw cuz they said they know it was someone from the side who look like you cuz because whoever did it didn't know there was cameras on that corner. They can't get a clear shot of the people who was there."

"Damn how many people was there?"

"Two they say but they say ya boy Flue Diz was talking to them niggas before it happened and they want to go pick him up, they say his footprints and his hair was at the scene and his face matched up with dudes but when they hollered at him, he said he didn't remember who he was talking to. Look I love you cuz if it was you I don't care and I don't want to know but what I'm asking is do you want me to holla at him before he get the chance to holla at someone else because he's their only lead besides the tape. The cops say they didn't really see their faces only their builds feel me."

Now Flue Diz was my man, one of the niggas from the hill I fuck with all like that and I just couldn't live with myself to say yeah about that.

"Look Ray J, I hope and pray this don't come back to bite me in my ass but I have to say I will pass on that one. That's my man and he's a good dude."

"No Doubt. But that's ya man don't let your heart get in the way about that time with no ending, smell me cuz."

"For sure."

"But just in case I put my man J Loc on him."

"Who J Loc the young wild nigga from Homewood?"

"Yeah L that him one call and it's dealt with."

Everybody from Pittsburgh knew about them Homewood niggas and how they get down and J was a monster. That dude right there was a loose cannon but if

he fucked with you, you were like family and he wouldn't backstab you. So I knew one leak about me it would be a wrap. Now as me and Ray J left that cold ass hospital and decided to run to homestead and go to TGI Fridays to get something to eat, I kept thinking about who tried to kill me. I mean they was all out about it too.

"Yo L you alright?"

"Naw cuz them niggas tried to kill me."

"Oh yeah cuz that lex truck you was talking about, that joint belongs to Spank Geez."

"Yeah?"

"And that nigga just copped a boat load of guns."

Come to find out that's that nigga Shady's peoples.

"Aint he from the county?"

"For sure he's from Manchester."

"Look call some of my niggas to let them know what happened then holla at a few niggas from Manchester we cool with and see if that small problem could get dealt with right in his circle."

"No Doubt cuz."

"And I got $100,000 for whoever cradle that nigga for me."

"I'll get on it cuz."

"But don't worry about it now, I'm out the hospital and I'm hungry."

"I hear you cuz."

CHAPTER 15

"Man fuck that nigga L-Roy, he had my cuz killed."

"Man you don't know that."

"Man ever since them indictments all the old heads with all the weight been booked and L-Roy took the side over and a million dollars was put on my peoples head. Now other than L-Roy who would put up that type of money?"

"That's true Spank but."

"But nothing hoe. And they didn't get along and Shady spanked his peoples."

"I'm just trying to tell that feuding with that nigga is like feuding with everybody because he aint with that gang shit and he's cool with a lot of people and that money talks."

"Fuck that nigga Rock, his money wouldn't mean nothing if he would've died the other day."

"All I'm saying you already let out a little anger and he don't know who you are so just fall back for a couple of months because he already put the word out to find that truck you got and they are going to be over every truck they see like that."

"You right, you right bro."

"So just fallback and go get a new whip."

"Yeah I did see this caddy truck I wanted."

"Come on lets go jump on it."

"Hey mom."

"What boy?"

"We out."

"We'll be out."

"I was just letting you know so you wouldn't be screaming and no one was here."

"Shaimar Grates Jenkins the third if you do not stop calling me when I'm watching my stories."

"Bye mom. Come on Rock let's roll."

"You got some green spank?"

"Yeah I got a zip of that kind bud left."

"Well I got some blunts in my whip cuz."

"Cuz ya ride is hot right now spank."

"Yeah true dat, true dat but rock."

"What's up?"

"It felt hella good dumpin that k on that nigga L-Roy dog."

"I know it did you was screamin and foamin at the mouth and shit."

"I wasn't that bad."

"Shit if you wasn't."

"You got that new killa in the whip?"

"You good at changing the subject aint you Spank."

"Man do you got that killa cam in the whip?"

"For sure."

"Well put that shit in and pound that shit because fuck losing weight I'm back on these streets movin cakes."

"You're shot out bro."

"Let's ride."

"Uncle Jerry how do you think this dress fits me."

"Tony if you don't come one girl. Well it's nice, I like it."

"For real Uncle Jerry?"

"I'm as for real as I can get."

"Ok then let's go."

"Look Tony were not going to Hawaii."

"Well where are we going?"

"To the mother land."

"Africa?"

"Yes ma'am."

"Hold on, hold on before you grab a ton of clothes, your new wardrobe will be on me."

"I'm fine with that."

"I bet you are, look Tony I have to go handle a few more things so I will meet you at the airport in about an hour. I will see you out front and if you don't see me, don't move because you probably beat me there. And anyway I will be calling you."

"I smell you."

"What's up with ya'll younger generation talking about I smell you."

"It's just a figure of speech Uncle Jerry."

"Well don't be smelling me, naw I'm just playing baby but I will see you in an hour. Bye bye girl."

"Bye, bye Uncle Jerry you crazy."

"Man get me some bbq chicken."

"Nigga you get it ya self you're a grown ass man."

"Come on L-Roy. You know I hate talkin to them crackers."

"You got to get out of that black power shit because green don't see no other color playa you feel me Ray J."

"Yeah I do but I don't play and dude look weird as fuck anyway."

"Alright I got you."

"Look cuz just get me the bbq chicken and shrimp with a baked potato and a glass of orange juice."

"All right as soon as they come over."

Hi how are you today? What can we get for you?"

"I will have the rib eye with rice and a side salad and some garlic bread and a glass of blue goose and my homie right here will have the bbq chicken and shrimp with a baked potato and a glass of sprite."

"Naw orange cuz."

"My bad. But if you would've told him it wouldn't be jacked up. And a glass of orange juice."

"Will there be anything else for you?"

"No that's all"

"Ok then your food will be out shortly."

Now as me and Ray J sit there and reflect on the good and bad times we had in this life. It's all different now because I'm rich and Ray J is my right hand man. The hood loves us but the dudes that was in the way hate us because we copin cakes when they're only buying cookies. It's funny how life just reveals everything.

As I get ready to get up and go to the bathroom, I see my Uncle Art. He was gone because the heat on the hood was so hot that if you were an old OG in the game they were taking you to jail. He's been gone almost 2 years.

"Hey Uncle Art."

"What's up boy, what are you doing here?"

"I figured I would come get a bite to eat before I head back to the Northside. You haven't been there in a while where you at?"

"You know Neff here and there until that heat fell off the hood somewhat."

"Hey how you doing Mr. Art?"

"Hey what's up Ray J.?"

"I heard you're that dude on the side now."

"Naw you couldn't heard that because I don't play with that game at all Unk."

"Yeah and my name aint Art."

"But it is and I don't fuck around but you could come sit at the table and bust it up with ya fam."

"Yeah I could do that."

I'm saying to myself what the fuck is going on, my Uncle is one grimy ass nigga and if he was out the way how did he know I was on and what the fuck is he doing here right now. It just didn't make no sense to me and I was going to get to the bottom of it. Now while we were eating it was quiet at the table and he never brought up how is the family or I'm sorry about ya mom and your brother. No nothing. He just talked about being that guy and that was it.

"Uncle Art did you go to my mom or my brothers funeral?"

"No son but I am still in pain about that, that's why I didn't bring it up."

"Yeah that's what's up."

"Do you know what happened to them?"

"No I didn't at the time but they say your mom was in a fire and your brother was kidnapped."

Now I heard that my brother called my Uncle Art before he died because Ray J's aunt was with my uncle at the time, she heard the whole conversation because my Uncle can't hear for shit and his phone was all the way up and everyone could hear his conversation. So I know he was lying because I was told my brother asked my Uncle to

pay the money but my he kept telling him he was broke and he don't even hustle and when it was all said and done whoever was there with T cursed out Art and Art hung the phone up. I never told anybody that, I was going to at least give him the benefit of the doubt and say he didn't know if they were setting him up or not. But no he keeps lying to me right to my face but see this time I'm not going to get anyone to handle this for me, this aint business this is personal and I have to put in my own work.

Now as I tap Ray J and walk with him to the door and let him know that I needed his gun. Ray J just laughed because he seen it coming.

"Look Ray J I'm a ride with Art and I will meet you downtown at the 7-11 right across the street from the Northside bus stop, man Ill just call you."

"Man be careful nut you know you just got out the hospital."

"Yeah I know that but this has to be handled."

"Just be careful cuz."

"You already know that. I'll be callin."

"For sure."

"Well Uncle Art I guess I'm with you know."

"Where ya friend go L-Roy?"

"Oh he had to handle some business so I told him you would drop me off on the Northside, that aint a problem

is it because I could call a cab or tell someone to come and get me."

"Naw Nephew it's cool."

"Good Look."

Now as we sit there and talk about fake old times, he never talked about how rich he was and how we were poor and he never even gave us a penny but it didn't matter. I was just waiting for him to finish his food so we could get this over with.

"So L-Roy you ready?"

"Yeah I'm ready."

"Well let's be out."

Before I even get in the car I pulled it out my pocket and put the chrome 32 in my right hand and pulled my hand inside my sleeve so when I hit him he won't have a chance to see what I'm doing and give him a chance to fight with me. Just empty it and roll out. Now we are on the highway and I'm wondering what exit is he going to take because if he takes the downtown exit I have to hit him downtown and that's going to be rough but if he takes the Northside exit I will have to hit him on the Northside and I don't want no more heat on the side than there already is and there are so many cameras on the Northside its crazy. Just as I thought he took the downtown exit and he was saying something to me but I was in another zone and when he stopped the car and asked me what was the matter with me and why I wasn't talking. I didn't see no

one through the rearview mirror so I put the gun to his face and I just started pulling right while he was in the middle of saying something, all six bullets emptied out into his face, he never had a chance and my ears were still ringing. I made sure I didn't touch anything and used my sleeved to touch everything. I dropped the gun on the seat and walked away while the car was sitting in the middle of the street. I pulled out my phone and started to smile as I called Ray J.

"Come on pick up the phone."

"Yo cuz, I'm already at the 7-11."

"What took you so long to answer the phone?"

"I was in there heating up this hotdog I bought this mozzarella cheese to put on top, now that's banging."

"Man just drive up to the Candy-Rama, I'm out in front."

No more than 2 seconds after I got off the phone the police came flying passed me, I knew where they were going and just couldn't wait to get up out of there.

CHAPTER 16

"Damn Uncle Jerry it took you forever to get here."

"But I am here aint I baby."

"Yes sir."

"Now come on let's take this flight."

"Do you have the tickets Uncle Jerry?"

"You know what Tony I knew I lost something."

"Stop playing all the time Uncle Jerry."

"Damn girl you don't have no sense of humor."

"That's because I'm already stressed out and we came all this way or should I say I came all this way and you didn't have the tickets, I would…"

"Before you get started Tony let's just get ready to board the plane."

"Ok Uncle Jerry but I wasn't going to say."

"Hush just come on baby because I didn't even hear a word you said."

"Come on get in cuz."

"It took you long enough."

"My bad bro."

"Look take me down my Aunt Matty's house."

"Where that at?"

"Down Hoodtown."

"Damn it's been that long."

"Yeah."

"Because I forgot."

"Just drop me off down there and tell Bay Bay or one of them young niggas to drop one of my rides off in front of the crib."

"I got you."

"No rush though. I'll be over here for a few."

"Alright."

Now I haven't been to see Mark's mom in years, she was no relation but I still cared for her and still called her my Aunt.

"Just hold on bro, let me make sure she's here." I got out the car and knocked on the door then the door opened.

"Hi Aunt Matty."

"L-Roy is that you?"

"Yes ma'am."

"Boy if you don't come here and give me a hug."

"Hold on Aunt Matty."

Now I ran back to the car told Ray J I was chillen and slammed the door. While Ray J was pulling out I ran straight in and hugged Aunt Matty. She felt so good in my arms, I felt like a kid again with a crush.

"So how's everything been going baby?"

"Pretty good. I'm sorry I haven't been down here sooner but I didn't know what to say to you."

"It's ok baby, I know you and Mark was tight baby."

"Look Aunt Matty you don't mind if I chill down here with you for a couple days."

"No I don't mind bae everything I have is yours."

"Thanks Aunt Matty."

"Oh I'm cooking right this second so I will talk to you in a few and everything is still the same way it was the last time you were here."

"Ok Aunt Matty."

As I watched her walk away, I seen she still had it. You could call me wild but she wasn't related to me and I cared about her something deeply. I mainly watched TV and ate the good food she was known to cook.

"Aunt Matty?"

"Yes baby?"

"Do you want to move?"

"Yes but my money aint right so I'm stuck baby."

"If you did have the money where were you thinking about leaving to?"

"Probably Fox Chapel."

"Are you sure?"

"Yeah it's nice out that way."

"And you still don't have no car?"

"No baby."

"Alright same thing if you had the money what type of car would you get?"

"Well I..."

"Hold on Aunt Matty. Did that sound like a horn?"

"No I didn't hear it baby."

"Hold on Aunt Matty let me see if that's my man out front."

"Go ahead."

I opened the door and screamed "Good luck little cuz."

"No doubt L, here go your keys."

"Who had the excursion?"

"Rudy had it. Ray J said he'll holla at you too cuz."

"Tell him I said alright."

"Be safe down here L. Call if you need me."

"No doubt lil cuz."

"Who was that?"

"Oh that was one of my young niggas bringing my truck down here."

"Wow that's nice L-Roy."

"Oh thank you."

"How much did that cost an arm and a leg I bet?"

"Naw not really. My homies put the rims, the grill and the tint on it all I did was buy it put the sounds in it and the TVs and that was free. Now what type of car did you say would get?"

"Probably a lex."

"What color?"

"Black."

"Why so dark?"

"I don't know baby."

"What about a pink Bentley coupe?"

"Well from what I was watching on that MTV show about them cars that's like $200,000."

"Yeah."

"But I would if I had the money."

"Well Aunt Matty I love you."

"I love you too L-Roy."

"I know that it's a little late now but tomorrow morning we going out Fox Chapel and get that house no matter what and we are going clothes shopping, get your nails and hair done, get that pink Bentley and buy you anything you want for that house."

"Now L-Roy I wish you were serious."

"Yeah I am, I'm rich Aunt Matty."

"Are you for real?"

"Yeah it's on and to keep it real with you I always wanted to do these types of things for you since I was a kid." Then I kissed her.

"L-Roy I never knew you felt like that then you just kissed me."

"I know it might feel strange but I want you in my life forever not as my fake Aunt but as my wife and I'm not taking no for an answer."

She broke down and just started crying.

"What's the matter Matty?"

"Well I feel the same about you too but what do you think everyone's going to say?"

"Man fuck all that I'm a grown ass man and you're a grown ass woman and we aint got no time to be thinking about them."

Then before I could finish she was all over me and I was all over her but tonight I wasn't fucking I was going to make love and I knew she felt the same too. We made love all night it was great, the best I ever had and I knew we were going on a journey and there was no turning back. The woman of my dreams and being with her I forgot I was even married but I have to come back to reality. But before that would happen I would make everything right first.

"Rudy, Rudy."

"What Bay Bay, damn you see me on the phone."

"Aint that nigga Spank Geezy right there? Yeah that's that bitch ass nigga slippin on the phone all crazy."

"I don't know Bay Bay."

"What don't you know that's him right there."

"But didn't L-Roy say he was going to get one of them Chester niggas to handle that."

"Man fuck all that L-Roy's my nigga this is handled. Spin the block I'll meet you on the corner."

"Hold up cuz, the police." But by the time Rudy got the words out Bay Bay was already at Spank Geezy's window unloading the K. Before Bay Bay knew it the police was telling him to drop the gun but he wasn't going out like that, he sent a few shots at the police then ran off. Rudy a homie until the end still picked him up on the corner and they were out. Shots rang off and Rudy was hit in the head while trying to get on the highway.

"Bro, bro wake up, what the fuck these dumbass pigs killed my bro."

Now as Bay Bay pulled Rudy out the driver's seat and took control of the wheel and still fired shots, he blacked out and crashed into a guardrail. He was shot also but the crash snapped him back into the fight he was up and running. He couldn't hear and he could barely see everything was so cloudy and blood was running down his face. He was trying his best to get away but he was moving so slow he turned and let off one last time before he passed out.

"So Matty you ready"

"Ready for what boy?"

"I told you we were going to get everything you want."

"Well I'm a little nervous."

"For what sexy?"

"Because I never did nothing like this before."

"It will be fine, don't worry about nothing. Now go ahead and get dressed with ya fat ass you know I like it."

"Oh I do."

"That why I want you to get dressed before I put something up in you."

"You're crazy but give me about an hour."

"For sure pretty lady."

Now as I'm chillen looking at the TV, I decided to call my man Shawn to my surprise he picked up on the second ring.

"Yo L-Roy, What up bro?"

"You alright?"

"Naw cuz, Rudy is dead and Bay Bay is fighting for his life."

"Hold on run this by me again."

"Look how I heard it is that Bay Bay and Rudy got at

Spank Geezy and the police was right there and they ended up getting into a shoot out with the police."

"Did the boy Spank Geezy live?"

"He's in critical condition too they say he got shot all in his face and a few limbs were hanging off. Whoever he was with died."

"Man where you at?"

"In the hood."

"Give me like 10 minutes and meet me at 7 court." Then I hung up the phone without even saying anything.

I got Matty and let her know what happened and told her that we had to hold on until tomorrow. I could tell she was sick but these were my niggas and I had to make sure everybody was alright. As I rode up to Northview, I thought about what really happened because Rudy don't ride like that, he'll shoot but cant anybody be around because he's scared to death to go to jail and he's humble so I know Bay Bay had to press him to do anything because he's a young hot head. That's my young nigga, he's a hot head and I love him so I needs him to pull through. When I hit the corner of 700 block of Mount Pleasant it was packed with people everywhere, women crying and dudes shooting their guns off, drunk and mad about what happened. So when I stepped out and tried to get everybody calm it was a little too late. Somebody already rode down bottom and shot the zone one police station up and caught one of the housing police up on Chicago Street and beat him down. It was crazy and I

knew Spank was going to pull through and go to the police because he would be scared on the street if I was out there. So I had to get him touched, I knew it was a lost cause but I was going to try.

"L-Roy."

"What up bro?"

"I'm fucked up right now."

"Cuz we all are. Did anyone go down to the hospital?"

"Yeah but the police aint letting no one holla at him, they say Bay Bay is going to pull through."

"You already call our lawyer?"

"Yeah he said he said he's going to get him a bond when they take him to see the judge."

"Alright and tell them niggas get at Spank."

"No doubt bro but it's going to be tough."

"Man you know that nigga aint about that as soon as he could talk the police will be coming to get niggas and you know they already on my heels so any little thing they coming to get me."

"Yeah L-Roy I feel you."

"So handle that."

"I got it dog, he's done, a dead man walking."

"That's what I want to hear."

"Look Shawn I got to go handle some business and I will get back."

"Cool."

"And keep these fools under control if the hood hot, I can't eat and if I can't eat Ima be hungry and if I'm hungry people aint going to like me."

"Be cool homie everything will be alright."

"I hope so but I'm out bro. Stay up."

"You too and be safe L and don't go cut a fool you got too much change for that."

Now as I get my roll on out of the hood I call Matty and tell her to get ready to go, that made her day because she thought the day was a wrap after what happened. So now I'm riding down Federal Street and three dudes jump out in front of my car. I was in la la land so I hit the brakes put the truck in park, jumped out and pulled my Glock 40 from my hip and flipped out.

"Yo is ya'll niggas crazy, I should hit one of ya'll niggas."

"Naw big cuz it aint even like that."

"Well what is it?"

"We worked for ya brother and we just wanted to know if we could work for you."

"Look meet me up the Heights tomorrow night around 9

or 10 o'clock but right now aint the time."

"Alright."

"My mans was killed and my young nigga is fighting for his life."

"We wasn't trying to get on your nerves we just be chasen money"

"Look ya'll good just be in the hood tomorrow night. Cool?"

"Yeah big cuz."

Now as I open the door to my truck I thought about how my mans mom would feel now that she lost her son but that was my homie and I would pay for everything and I wanted to be done this time for real. The game was crazy but it wasn't the dope game itself it was life and it was time for me to slide to the side. But it's the rush and the power, the respect, the everything that the game was and is to every hustler and gangster and con man that holds me there. As I rode to Matty's house my phone rang.

"Yo L."

"Who's this?"

"Your wife."

"Damn."

"Damn what L-Roy you haven't been home in days."

"Look Sharon I'm going through something right this

second."

"Well whatever it is bae we could go through it together. It aint like we aren't from the same hood, I know what happened and I'm sorry baby but you have a family at home who loves you."

"Look I will be home tonight and we will talk."

"That's all I ask, just talk to me L-Roy, tell me how you feel and if you still love me and if I'm doing something wrong let me know."

"Naw it's just that I be stressed about a lot of shit that's going on out here and my mind be going, going crazy baby but I will be home soon so just be cool K."

"Yeah L."

"But I do love you."

"I love you too L with all my heart."

"Bye baby."

"Bye L."

I hang up the phone and finish my drive down Matty's. I stopped and made a few sales down Hoodtown. I know I didn't need it but they did so I gave them something to remember me. I pull up to the house and I could see that the door was open and the screen door was off. I tuned the engine off and reached for my hip as I went carefully and was down low and held my gun in both hands like I was the police or something. I looked around

and saw no one was there and the house looked trashed like someone was looking for something then my phone rang. Now I was a little worried because the number was blocked but I answered anyway.

"Yo who's this?"

"Matty."

"What the fuck happened?"

"Look L I went to the store to get some smokes and on the way back I saw the door was open and the screen was all fucked up. I decided to look in and seen a few guys running around so I went down the street to my friends house. I was still shook up that's what took me so long to call you."

"It's ok bae, Ima call somebody to fix this door and get somebody to clean up then we're out ok."

"Ok L."

"Well call me back in about an hour."

"I'm cool with that L."

"Bye baby."

"Bye boo."

Now the hoods hot as fish grease and I'm the main young nigga bringing that work in and if this nigga Spank Geezy make it might be a rap for the kid. So I grabs Matty up and we go get a condo in Miami then I come back get

Sharon and move her down ATL making sure my baby will be safe and make sure Bay Bay would be able to get out of jail on house arrest, make sure he got one of them top notch lawyers on his case.

Now Spank Geezy's hospital room gets fire bombed and they can't get that nigga out on time he gets burned up. Slowly but surely I'm cutting all my ties from Pittsburgh but not before I pay a few more people some visits. This one was personal and had to be done by me. I told you in the beginning a few people I was close too would have to die.

I moved locations and I'm getting money out of Columbus Ohio, I got a nice team and they're getting money both Me and Jerry. My connect is cool but he keeps raising prices on me like I'm sweet.

"Yo Jerry."

"Hey what up L-Roy."

"You know same old thing. I got this record company moving fast on me and my cd sales are growing."

"Well how many you moving out the trunk."

"About 500 cds."

"Ok what you selling them for?"

"For about 12 a whop."

"Naw that's too much."

"I was only trying to get rid of them for about 10."

"Naw that's too cheap especially with the quality of music you got."

"Oh ok well I'm a holla at you in a few hours."

"Alright be safe."

"No doubt."

That right there is how me and Jerry communicate over the phone when we are talking about that work. Every cd is a key and I need 500 hundred of them at 10 thousand a whop. But he talking about the powdered is so good that he wants 12 thousand a key but I'm like fuck it because I turn every key into 2 keys but that's more money out my pocket. Instead of paying 5 million I would be paying him like 6 million and that's crazy. So I called up a few youngsters to take this trip to NC with me to pick up work from my connect but I have been working on something since I've been in Columbus.

I became friends with this lady, and no we are not fucking there's no need to smash every chick, her name is Amber and she goes to school for computer drafting. She's been playing around on the computer since she was a kid and she loves money too. She has found a way to make counterfeit bills; I'm a hustler so you know I could find something to do with that. Oh yeah out here they call me Polo not L-Roy.

"Hello Polo."

"Hello Amber. What's the project lookin like youngin?"

"It's going well." She says. "10 million dollars was a lot of work."

"But the time was worth the $500,000 I'm giving you."

"No doubt Polo."

"Now look on the passenger side of my ride is the money, did you park your car anywhere around here?"

"No because my friend dropped me off and I told him you would take me home."

"Who Paul?"

"Yes."

"Man he's a rat don't be telling dude what I be doing."

"I don't."

"Well."

"Well what Polo?"

"Where your part of the deal at?"

"Oh it's at the crib."

"Well let's ride. Oh yeah, go ahead and drive the Chrysler. Ima take my truck."

"On the way over there I was all geeked up listening to that project pat with twelve twelve's in my excursion wit 2

eighteens and 4 amps, 4 batteries all made by Bose. I was killing the game, vest on, mac 90 on my back seat, my side panels and windows bulletproof, I was in the game. Ya'll know how I used to be about being flashy not anymore it's a cake walk out here. Look my excursion is lime green with gold flakes with gold mirror tint and sittin on 27 inch 100 spoke hammers wit shaved door handles, low probes, everything digital, 7 TVs in it and with leather seats with Polo stitched in them with gold stitching, playstation 3's the whole nine.

Now the whole plan is to burn Uncle Jerry with 6 million of this counterfeit money, he's not going to look at it but when he figures it out he's going to send them niggas for me. And yes he does know where I live at but that's the least of my worries. I just hope he don't pick tomorrow to look in this fucking bag or it's on. It took 3 months to put this shit together.

As I get on the phone to call Amber, my phone rings and the number is blocked but I answer it anyway. "Hello?"

"Yes how are you doing Mr. Gray?"

"Who's this?"

"An old friend of yours, you might know me as Detective Jones and my friend as Detective Faulk."

"Well how did ya'll get this number?"

"Your friend Bay Bay gave it to us."

"Fuck!" I scream into the phone.

All of a sudden my truck is surrounded by DEA, FBI, Homicide and ATF. I wasn't going out like that. I was ready to reach for the mac 90 but if they didn't have anything on me they would then. So I just gave up like fuck it.

CHAPTER 17

Bay Bay if you testify on L-Roy we'll give you immunity."

"I have no problems with that. And Detective Jones?"

"Yes."

"How long before I could be out?"

"As soon as you sign these papers."

"For sure."

As Bay Bay gets out on an OR bond and makes it back to the streets, I have been questioned and charged with 2 counts of homicide, 10 counts of reckless endangerment, 1 count of conspiracy and the inquest date was 10 days after that. Deif and Wymer were called to handle my case.

I can't believe this shit is all I keep saying while I'm in the county. I mean I'm cool all in all but I don't want to be

here. I snuck in a half ounce of strawberry haze & wraps and I was about to go hard on it. I had 9 stacks on my books and a $100 bill I snuck in so I bought a lighter from one of the block workers. I rolled up a few blunts and I was good to go. About 2 or 3 in the morning I was told to pack it up, I figured it was some bullshit and I started asking some questions.

"For what?"

"Because Mr. Gray the CO said you are leaving."

I left all that shit in the room hit the button and jetted to the door.

"Mr. Gray you have to put your blankets in the white bucket."

I ran back grabbed them, threw them in the bucket and waited for the relief officer to come and get me. This fool took like 10 minutes so I cussed his bitch ass out.

"Hey man, I'm out of here don't ever take that long to come and get me again."

"Or what tough guy?"

"I'll beat the shit out of you pussy." He got quiet.

We make our way down to the ground floor; I sat in this room for about 15 minutes then put my clothes on.

"Mr. Gray, Mr. Gray."

"Yeah what's crackin?"

"We won't be able to give you your money right now but we will send a check to your house."

"Well how much is it?"

"$25.00."

"Well don't worry about it."

I knew right then and there they thought I was my old head from the way; he had the same name and an almost identical DOC number. I was home free. I went back in this other little room near the officer's station for about 10 minutes and I just realized I had no money or my phone.

"Come on guys." The guard says as he opens the door to let us out.

"Follow me." As he drops me off to another guard who takes us up on the elevator to the main floor. I get out of the elevator and go outside, all I could think about was money and a phone.

"Hey homie you trying to cop some weed?" I asked this dude standing outside. He looked like he had some change with his white mink on, a Versace outfit and some gators. I kind of figured he was just waiting on someone.

"Naw dog not really but what kind of nolia you got?"

"Some strawberry dro and strawberry wraps."

"Damn homie I never tried that before. Well what you want?" He says.

"Like 50 a gram."

"Damn."

"But look this is what I'll do; I'll give you half of this for 300."

"All that for 3?"

"Yeah."

"Deal."

Now I got $300 but no phone until I see this lil white ugly muthafucka on the phone and just snatch his shit.

"Hey what are you doing asshole?" I smacked the shit out of him then ran off.

Now I don't got shit in the burg but I'm glad they didn't take me to no jails in Ohio or I would still be locked up. As I think about who to call, I'm just thinking about I aint got shit in the Burgh so I did the unthinkable I ask some lady at the bus stop for change for a dollar and waited for the bus.

"What's crackin Bay Bay?" As he pulls up to the 700 block of Mount Pleasant.

"You know you know chillen."

"Damn cuz one of the lil homies say you just cop that whip."

"No doubt lil nigga, you know niggas from the heights gotta stay fly cuz."

"Aint no question locsta."

"Well, I just got out lil homie and I'm fiending for some of that nolia."

"Oh lil project got some."

"Well go find him and I'll be right here and here's a dub for ya time cuz."

"Good look." As lil homie mumbles something and walks away.

CHAPTER 18

"Do this bus got to the Northside?" I ask while I'm getting on the bus behind this old lady who smells like she's been outside her entire stay on this planet.

"Yes it does."The bus driver replies "It goes to East Ohio Street then back downtown."

"Thanks big fella."

I look around and I see if I'm going to sit or stand and I see a nice young lady in the back that I'm a try to holla at. I'm getting thrown everywhere as I walk to the back like we are hitting big ass potholes and I'm bumping into all types of people smelly, weird and some people who liked me running into them. I finally made it to the back and I was already smiling at her then unexpectedly she spoke.

"Hi Laron."

I'm saying to myself how this fine ass girl know me. I replied "What's up bae" While sitting down next to her. She was talking but I couldn't even hear her. You have to understand she was immaculate, light green eyes, long jet black hair, her tone was like a creamy tan, she looked Italian or something, her body was a 20 plus, right size breasts like a c cup, her legs were oiled down with this tiny mini skirt on that looked like if she sneezed all her goods would be exposed.

"Laron, Laron." She says as she's hitting me on the shoulder breaking me out of my daze.

"Whatup."

"I see you still do that."

"What?"

"Don't listen when someone's talking to you."

"Naw it aint like that cutie."

"And you better not have been lusting off me, I know you're nasty."

"Now for one call me L-Roy please my mom is the only one who calls me by my first name and she passed away. Second what is your name and where do you know me from?"

"My name is Laneia and I'm from out the Duke and you used to talk to my cousin Tony. I used to talk to you on the phone all the time."

"Oh yeah I remember but how did you know what I look like?"

"Well usually when I came over it was early in the morning and you were knocked out butt naked in front of the TV so I seen all of you, I kinda got used to seeing your naked ass."

"I bet you did and you got the nerve to call me nasty."

"Well you know a woman has to have her fun too."

"Ok well where you about to go Laneia?"

"Over to Stedeford's on the Northside to pick up a few cds then go to the aviary then back downtown to go shopping. What about you?"

"Well first I'm a get your phone number then I'm a think about you all day then I'm a go to sleep then when I wake up I'm a call you."

"You're crazy L-Roy but I look forward to hearing from you so just give me one second so I could find my pen and paper then I got you."

"Aww aren't you so nice Laneia."

"Well you know L-Roy I try to do what I could when I could do it."

"Man you got that shit off me punk."

"Nope L-Roy, just made it up."

When she finished writing her number down I snatched it

off her and she just stopped smiling.

"Well nasty man here goes our stop."

"That's what it look like."

"I wish." Before she got a chance to finish I put a wet one on her lips.

"Now think about that and I'll call you tomorrow." I ran off the bus.

"Bay Loc, what's crackin cuz."

"Project the neighborhood superstar."

"You know me playa. So what you need cuz?"

"What you got?"

"Well I got 3 flavas for ya crippin. I got some blueberry haze, some apple dro, some of that kush."

"That's nice, real nice. Just give me a zip of all 3."

"No question. Just give me like 10 minutes oh yeah before I walk away I just rolled up a blunt of that apple so enjoy it until I come back."

"Yeah I needs that."

Now as project walked away from Bay Bay and Bay Bay sparked that blunt he got back in his car and rolled his window up, turned his ac on low, put some of that killa on, put his seat back and enjoyed the blunt.

"Damn I need my phone, I can't remember nobody's number. Fuck it. I'm a just get a jitney up."

As I get my jog on to the jitney station stuff just hit me like a ton of bricks, losing my mom, my brother, now they're trying to take my life away, what should or could I do. Now as I jog passed Allegheny General my eyes start to water because I start thinking about my lil bro but I had to shake it. He was gone, I was still here and I'm a hold it down. I couldn't believe I even had a kid, shit was just movin real fast. I make a right on Boil street a lot of neighborhood kids ran up and started asking me for money so I just threw like $50 in the air and screamed out get it how ya'll live. I finally made it to the jitney station there were no cars in, I'm mad as hell looking around even going downstairs into the jitney station but no one was around. Then Prince pulled up.

"Yo Prince what up, you still jitneying?"

"No doubt." The ugly wanna be fly African man says.

I jumped in gave Prince a $5 bill and told him to keep the change. I felt a blunt in my pocket I must've rolled down at the county so I ask Prince did he want to hit this blunt and he said yeah because most of them Africans smoke weed. The ride was silent except for Prince keep choking off that strawberry and asking me where I got the weed from.

"I got that out Ohio."

"Yeah Yeah."

Before he could ask me anymore questions we was already across the bridge to my hood and I seen one of my young niggas at the booth tryin to holla at one of them chicks. I told prince this was cool and I jumped out leaving him the weed. I heard him screaming out at me but I kept walking then he finally caught on.

"Yo what's crackin?" I say to one of my young niggas after getting in his car and startling him.

"What's up L-Roy, where you come from?"

"A long story, look drive me up on Mount Pleasant."

"No doubt cuz." "Alright shorty." He says to the lil chick after pulling off.

"What happening L-Roy?"

"You know getting that change."

"I know that's why I been trying to holla at you."

I cut his conversation short and asked did he have his burner on him.

"Naw cuz, it's over projects crib that where all the burners be at when we in the hood."

"Well take me there."

"No question because I'm tryin to get a queey of that kush, smell me cuz."

I laughed as I told cuz I smell him. As we hit the block I see project about to come out his crib so I jumps out the

whip and ask project for a strap.

He asked me "What you want cuz?"

"Something that spit cuz, already loaded."

"I got this tec 22 right there for you cuz already loaded and everything."

"Where?"

"Right under the pillow. This tec is sweet cuz wit an extended clip and everything."

"How many shots it hold?"

"Like 50 cuz."

"Yeah?"

"For real L that thing spits. But what you got some beef or something?"

"Yeah some nigga ratting on me I got to handle him."

"No doubt cuz, no doubt. I'm about to walk around 700 block to make this snap walk wit me cuz you know niggas miss you."

"Alright cuz just for you. Naw I'm jokin I was going to walk around and chill for a minute anyway. Well let's ride."

"Hold up L-Roy I almost forgot about lil homie out front."

"Handle that Ima just walk slow."

On my way down to 700 block I was walking through the park and forgot I had the tec out until some old head screamed out.

"L-Roy I know you aint about to start trippin."

"Naw why you say that for?"

"Because you walking wit cha gun out, well you better put that away."

"Good look Unk." So I put it in front of my pants.

Niggas was coming over to me giving me daps and asking me all types of questions that I wasn't really answering I was just laughing and nodding and I kept saying you know that's how I do it. Before I seen this black 3 series sitting on chrome and tinted out, project bumped me as he ran passed me.

"Come on L-Roy." As he ran over to the car.

I seen he pointing back at me talking to whoever was in the car. I was like 3 feet away from the car before I asked project who was in there.

"You know who it is L-Roy the number one stunna Bay Bay."

Before I could even blink I was reaching and telling project to get out the way, I let off like 10 shots before running up to the car. Now his window is cracked and exposing him I let off more shots while he tried to reach up under his seat where his hammer probably was. But before that I had to at least let off 30 more shots before he

tilted over. I used my T-shirt to open his door and put the rest in his head but nothing it was jammed and I was trying to un-jam it. I guess in the mist of my rage I didn't let off the trigger enough or something. Now as I stand there looking at this lifeless body I say to myself aint nothing going to stop me now until he turned and looked at me. It was like slow motion then I seen a gun it looked like a chrome nine. Shots rang off I was hit in my shoulder and in my back. I guess he wasn't dead and it wasn't over because the fat lady never sang....

ABOUT THE AUTHOR

My name is James Freeman but where I am from everyone calls me big Nicc or Nitty the great. I am from the 700 block of Mount Pleasant road in Northview Heights, which is a housing project in the City of Pittsburgh, Pennsylvania. I grew up hard and in poverty but we made do with what we had. My life style got me money, women and a prison sentence. I've been down 12 years now for a homicide I caught back in 2002. My life has always been a tail-spin but they streets have taught me a lot. That is why I am able to give you some of the street stories and wars because I have lived them first hand. Now you know a little about me. This is what I do; I'll have more books coming out soon, be on the lookout for my next book Killa, and make sure you grab them all. Much love and respect for everyone who got my book and know this is only the beginning.